THE SPECTRAL MIST

THE SPECTRAL MIST

CLARISSA ROSS

THORNDIKE
CHIVERS

This Large Print edition is published by Thorndike Press®, Waterville, Maine USA and by BBC Audiobooks, Ltd, Bath, England.

Published in 2005 in the U.S. by arrangement with Maureen Moran Agency.

Published in 2005 in the U.K. by arrangement with the author.

U.S. Hardcover 0-7862-7234-1 (Romance)
U.K. Hardcover 1-4056-3252-6 (Chivers Large Print)
U.K. Softcover 1-4056-3253-4 (Camden Large Print)

The text of this Large Print edition is unabridged.
Other aspects of the book may vary from the original edition.

Set in 16 pt. Plantin by Al Chase.

Printed in the United States on permanent paper.

British Library Cataloguing-in-Publication Data available

Library of Congress Cataloging-in-Publication Data

Ross, Clarissa, 1912–
    The spectral mist / Clarissa Ross.
        p. cm.
    ISBN 0-7862-7234-1 (lg. print : hc : alk. paper)
    1. Married women — Fiction.   2. California — Fiction.
3. Recluses — Fiction.   4. Mansions — Fiction.   5. Uncles
— Fiction.   6. Poets — Fiction.   7. Large type books.
I. Title.
PR9199.3.R5996S67 2005
813′.54—dc22   2004056962

To the memory of Walter Fultz, editor and friend, who gave me help and encouragement and published my first mystery short story many years ago.

CHAPTER ONE

From the moment Enid Blair saw Cliffcrest rising like some phantom structure out of the thick gray mist, a macabre mood had come over her. The sight of its towering square hulk of green with white trim wreathed in the fog had at once suggested mystery and horror to her. And once she was within its baroque, mansarded walls she was to discover that she had not been wrong. She was to learn that everyday living in the old mansion on the California cliffs was filled with mystery and, concealed by the calm facade of its people, was a horror she'd never dreamed could exist!

When she'd entered the art gallery at the corner of Madison and Eighty-First Street in New York City on that August afternoon she'd not guessed that among its patrons would be her future husband. Nor could she have known that within a few weeks he would whisk her away to a new home on the California coast midway between Los Angeles and San Francisco. She had gone to the art auction of Chinese prints on behalf of her lawyer employer, who did not have the time to attend and who trusted her judgment.

Trusted it enough to give her permission to write a check for up to five figures for any object or objects she saw that struck her fancy. So here she was elbowing her way into the small street level gallery whose chairs were already almost all taken. She knew the auctioneer, Mr. Zacharias, a small man with a dignified face and a trim white beard. He nodded and smiled to her as she took a chair. At the moment he was engaged in a conversation with a tall, slim serious-faced blond man.

The two parted and the blond man took a chair not far from hers. For just a moment he glanced up from his catalogue to eye her with interest. His gaze was so keen she blushed slightly and speculated on what Mr. Zacharias might have said to him about her. The old art dealer knew her from previous auctions and often teased her about her beauty. Enid had a modest opinion of her looks. But in a sketch drawn of her by an artist friend of her employer's she had come out vibrant, green-eyed and red-haired with an enigmatic smile. She thought it looked like her but flattered her in that her face was wider than the frail one depicted by the artist.

The most valuable painting to be offered that day was a Li T'ang study of a summer landscape. And this would undoubtedly be bid for by one of the various museums. The price would be fantastic. But there were many prints and paintings of later Chinese artists which might be available to the private collector. It was for one of these she was looking. And she assumed the willowy blond man might be doing the same thing.

The auction began quietly and just as she'd expected the Li T'ang painting went to a Midwestern museum. Then the less valuable items were offered and she bid on one titled "The Long River". It did not surprise her that the chief contender for the lovely painting was the blond young man. And it was he who finally outbid her. It was the end of the auction as far as she was concerned. None of the other items seemed suitable for her employer.

At an intermission in the proceedings auctioneer Zacharias came to her. The little man had a twinkle in his blue eyes as he smiled and said, "I'm sorry you didn't get the Shan Hu painting, but rest assured it went to good hands."

Enid was on her feet to leave. "I'm glad of that."

"Allow me to introduce you to Mr.

Geoffrey Hunt," the auctioneer said as the blond young man joined them with an apologetic smile. "This is Miss Enid Blair who has attended many of these events."

"You are fortunate, Miss Blair," the young man said in a pleasant voice. "I'm only in New York occasionally. This is a treat for me."

"Where do you make your home?" she'd asked.

He said, "Not far from Carmel in California. Do you know the West Coast?"

"As a visitor only," she told him. "But I think the Carmel area is truly beautiful. The great rocky shoreline fascinated me."

Geoffrey Hunt nodded. "In spite of oil spills and the like we do have a lot of natural beauty left."

Mr. Zacharias chuckled. "While in New York City we make no claims to any. Unless you count beautiful people as an ecological resource. And I maintain we have the world's largest share of them."

Geoffrey Hunt was studying Enid with that odd intentness again. Solemnly, he said, "I agree. And I suggest that Miss Blair is a good example."

"Come," she laughed. "No need to placate my feelings for losing the painting by flattery."

"I mean it," he said. "Are you staying for the rest of the auction?"

"No," she said.

"Then let's leave together and have a drink somewhere," he suggested.

Mr. Zacharias beamed on them. "Sounds like an excellent idea. I'll have your purchase made ready for shipping in a few days, Geoffrey."

"Thank you," the slim young man said with a smile as he took Enid's arm to see her out.

They hailed a taxi outside the gallery and he took her to the Palm Court of the Plaza Hotel. There they found a secluded table hidden from the main room by a marble column and Geoffrey ordered their drinks. The orchestra had begun the regular afternoon concert and it was a highly desirable atmosphere in which to relax. In no time they were Geoffrey and Enid to each other and busy filling in each other on their backgrounds.

"I'm only acting for my employer," she told him across the table. "Don't think I'm any wealthy young woman collector. I'm a plain personal secretary."

Geoffrey laughed and she was struck by his perfect white teeth and the way they contrasted with his bronzed face. He said,

"Please don't get any ideas I'm a million-aire, either. I was at the sale representing my uncle. You've probably heard of him, Ford Hunt."

Her eyebrows lifted. "Not *the* Ford Hunt? The famous poet?"

"That's right," he said. "He won the Pulitzer Prize about ten years ago. He doesn't write as much now but he published a book of poems last year. And he's going to have another ready for the publisher in a few months."

"But his poetry is terrific!" she exclaimed. "So sensitive and yet with such a broad appeal." She frowned. "I seem to remember he experienced some sort of tragedy and he's been a kind of recluse since then."

Geoffrey's face shadowed. "You're right. My uncle has made no public appearances lately. In fact he lives a hermit-like existence in his big house in Carmel. His wife killed herself plunging from a balcony of the house onto the rocky beach below. It changed him completely."

"How awful for him," she said, sadly. "And he is one of the most venerated literary figures in America." She had a mental picture of the stern-faced, white-haired man whose likeness she'd seen so many times. He had read a poem of his at a Presidential inauguration and stood out a lonely, sincere figure raising his voice against pride, violence and greed.

"I have shared the tragedy in a way," Geoffrey told her. "I act as his personal secretary. I'm about the only link he has with the outside world these days. He lives in an apartment at the attic level of Cliffcrest and besides an elderly servant and myself, no one sees him. Not even his lawyer who looks after his business affairs and lives in the house. Nor my mother and brother who also live there. Uncle Ford likes to have the family near him but now he refuses to see any of them but me."

"Has this been going on long?"

"Since his wife's suicide. We hope that one day it will change."

"I should think so," she said. "Ford Hunt is too great a man to live that way."

"I agree," Geoffrey said seriously. "At several periods in his life he's had minor breakdowns but never anything like this."

"Wasn't his wife a much younger woman?" Enid asked.

"Yes," he said. "She was his second wife. His first died years ago. The second wife married him in relative old age. That probably was a mistake. They seemed happy enough at first, but I believe his increasing irascibility brought on her depression and eventually her suicide."

"A sad business."

"I have witnessed it all at close range," Geoffrey said with a grave look on his lean, bronzed face. "It's a tragedy. Sometimes I blame the house. Cliffcrest is a rather ugly old place perched out on the cliffs. A kind of Victorian monstrosity with a mansarded style and two tall brick chimneys streaking up to the sky. Uncle Ford picked it because it has so much space, more than twenty-four rooms. And I find the size of it depressing."

She smiled over her drink. "At least you have lots of space to live in."

"We have that," he agreed. The violin and piano music provided a pleasant background to their talk. He said, "Away from Cliffcrest I forget what it's really like there. Perhaps that is good."

"I'm sure it is," she agreed. "We all need change."

"I'm sure you're right," he said, his eyes meeting hers. "I want to enjoy my vacation in New York. I hope we may be able to see each other again."

She gave him a teasing smile. "You mean to follow me to other art auctions and take the best offerings away from me?"

14

"Nothing like that," he assured her. "I want to see you on a personal basis. I've enjoyed meeting you."

"It's been pleasant for me as well," she assured him.

And so that afternoon at the Palm Court began a whirlwind series of meetings between them. As Geoffrey's time in New York became short they met every evening. And it was on one of these last evenings when they sat in the lounge of the Rainbow Grill that he discussed the future seriously with her.

They were seated by a window overlooking the lights of Manhattan in the dimly lit lounge. In the blue shadows of the room she could barely see Geoffrey's handsome profile. And the couples at the other tables around them were lost in the near-darkness, giving them a feeling of being alone.

Geoffrey said simply, "I don't want to leave you."

"We'll meet again."

"How can I be sure?" he worried. "There are so many daily pressures. I don't know when I'll get back to New York. And you have no plans of visiting California?"

"Not at the moment," she admitted, though the parting was just as difficult for her as it was for him. She had come to like Geoffrey in the short time they'd known each other. Perhaps she even loved him.

"I don't know what to say," he confessed. "I'd like to ask you to marry me right away. But then I think of Cliffcrest, Uncle Ford and the others living there. It is a grim place to think about taking a bride."

Enid stared at him thoughtfully. "And you must take whoever you marry there?"

"Yes," his reply was emphatic. "I have no choice. Uncle Ford is too dependent on me for me to think of leaving. It may go on that way until after his death. Then only will I be free."

She stared at him. "That's not a happy prospect."

"No," he agreed. "But I can't desert him."

"Ford Hunt is a wonderful man," she said. "I can understand why you feel you must give him full loyalty."

"There's no question about it," he said unhappily. "He needs me. I'm taking a chance staying here this long. Of course I phone every day. That keeps me somewhat in touch."

She showed concern. "What has the word been?"

"I only hear from his manservant," Geoffrey said. "As far as I can tell from him he's well enough but not doing any writing in my absence. That is bad because he is

16

behind schedule now and he should get the copy to the publisher on time."

"Would they mind waiting?"

"He's already had an extension. I think they would be upset. And then there's the matter of money. Famous as my uncle has become, the early days were difficult for him financially. He needs to amass a good sum to see him through his old age."

"Of course," she agreed. It seemed to her that Geoffrey was the very epitome of the devoted nephew.

"And my good fortune is tied in with my uncle's," he went on. "I gave up my engineering work to act as his secretary. At the time he'd just recovered from one of his health breakdowns and no one else seemed to be able to reach him. I managed to get him working again. But now my financial future is tied with his."

"And the others in your family also live with him," she said.

"Yes. Mother is a widow and has taken charge of Uncle Ford's house. My brother, Peter, had a start on an excellent musical career. He's a talent in his own right as a folk singer. But he got into drugs and his career collapsed. He's supposed to be cured of his addiction but his talent seems to have vanished. He lives at Cliffcrest and plays

17

piano in a small roadside bar near the town. It's no kind of job for him but it's all he seems to want or be able to do."

"I'm sorry," she said. "Is he younger than you?"

"By four years," Geoffrey said. "Francis James has an apartment in the house. He's Uncle Ford's lawyer and business manager. He's a sharp business person and so quiet you'd hardly guess he was in the house. Then there's Watts, he's my uncle's man-servant who has been with him for more than a decade. Outside of these people there are a few regular servants."

"It's not such a large group of people to live in that big house," she said.

"No. Still, temperaments sometimes collide," he said. "And there is a kind of tension from Uncle Ford being up there alone and unseen and yet having a kind of control over all of us."

"Do the reporters still bother him for interviews?" she asked.

"No. They've given up. He refuses to see anyone. Occasionally he gives a written statement to be distributed to the media and that's it."

"Still, you must be very proud of him. Just to know someone close to Ford Hunt thrills me."

"You feel strongly about him?"

"Yes," she said, "I'd say I do. He's one of the century's great talents."

Geoffrey leaned across the table so that his earnest face became clearer to her in the shadows. "Do you revere him enough to marry me and live at Cliffcrest even though you might have to sacrifice some privacy and full claim on me?"

It was a startling question and thought-provoking. She knew Geoffrey liked her but she'd not expected a proposal. Now she had to give him an answer. She said, "I'd prefer to begin marriage alone with the man I loved. But I suppose there are circumstances where this is not possible."

"Cliffcrest is not a happy house," he warned her. "Many times its people are in conflict. And yet I must live there as long as I'm dedicated to Ford Hunt and keeping his talent alive."

She was to remember these words and think of them later. At the time she accepted them as a young, idealistic man's willingness to make a sacrifice for a talented uncle.

She said, "I think I admire your determination."

"You haven't said whether you'll marry me or not."

"And live at Cliffcrest?"

"That has to be part of it."

Enid hesitated. There was a small inward voice which warned her against the move. Which told her she was risking great unhappiness. But balancing this was the honesty of Geoffrey's attitude and his quiet, unassuming love for her.

She said, "Very well, Geoff. I'll marry you if you wish."

He reached out and took her hand. "You really mean it?"

"Yes."

"It will mean marrying right away and returning to Cliffcrest fairly shortly."

She laughed. "If I'm to indulge in madness why not go all the way?"

"Wonderful," he enthused as he bent forward to kiss her.

And so it was settled. And the wild preparations which precede any marriage began. There was the notifying of her mother, remarried in Florida. The sad business of telling her boss and giving up the job which she'd enjoyed. Telling close friends and arranging for them to be at the wedding in the tiny downtown chapel and at the St. Moritz afterward for the reception.

Geoffrey was busy with getting the license, the clergyman and the other details of the wedding settled. He also kept in touch with California. He'd told his family about the marriage but none of them were able to get away to be with them at this important moment.

"Uncle Ford will write a special poem for us later," Geoffrey promised.

She tried to learn from him how his mother and the others felt about the match but he gave her no information. She came to the conclusion that they were not overjoyed. And she determined to win them over when she arrived at Cliffcrest. Surely she could somehow make them like her!

They planned to honeymoon in New York at the Plaza Hotel. She had her apartment subleased to a friend and so all those details were settled. When they left New York she would be free of all her associations there and ready to begin a new existence. A good life, she hoped. After all, how could it be otherwise with Geoffrey as her husband?

The wedding was a happy one. And so were the honeymoon days that followed at the Plaza. They strolled hand in hand in the park like the other young lovers, went to concerts and the theatre in the evenings and danced at the Café Pierre until the small hours almost every night.

Then came the fateful phone call from California which changed it all and ended their honeymoon. It was from the lawyer, Francis James. Enid had no idea what the conversation was about. But when Geoffrey put the phone down he told her, "We have to return to Cliffcrest at once."

She stared at him, worried. "Nothing bad has happened?"

"No," he said in a curt fashion foreign to him. "But my uncle isn't well and he's just sitting moping around. His lawyer thinks I should get back at once. I'm the only one he'll pay any attention to."

"We had another four days planned here," she reminded him. "We have tickets for shows."

"We'll return them to the broker or give them to some of your friends," Geoffrey said with a weary look on his bronzed face. "We must leave."

She rose from her chair with a sigh. "Very well. When?"

"Next plane we can book for the West Coast."

"I'll pack then," she said, resigned to it, though disappointed.

Geoffrey suddenly showed a tenderness. He came and took her in his arms. "I'm sorry, darling. But I warned you it could be hard at times. I didn't try to deceive you."

"No," she said, managing a wan smile. "You told me the worst."

"This is a minor crisis," he said. "Uncle Ford will be fine as soon as I get to Cliffcrest."

"I hope so," she said. "And I hope your family will like me."

"They'll love you just as I do," he told her and he kissed her gently as if to underline it.

The hurried departure from the hotel and the air trip to the West Coast became blurred memories for her. A chauffeur waited for them in a black limousine at Carmel. And her apprehensions began as they drove the last mile of the foggy private road to reach Cliffcrest. She saw its grim outline through the mist — and worried.

There was something about the isolated old house on the cliff and its grounds that sent a tiny chill of fear through her. And she couldn't explain why. She leaned close to Geoffrey as they got out of the limousine and she stared up at the four-story rambling mansion.

"It's overpowering," she gasped. "Unbelievable!"

"Built by a railroad tycoon a hundred years ago," her husband said. "He soon tired of it and sold it. Since then it has passed through many hands until Uncle Ford bought it."

"I suppose it's ideal for him," she said. "He needs to be away by himself and quiet."

Geoffrey smiled down at her. "Only the roar of the waves on the beach to bother you here."

They walked toward the front verandah and entrance. She noticed the wide lawns and to the right a weathervaned coachhouse which now probably was used as a garage or gardener's outbuilding. There wasn't a sign of a person around, other than themselves. Everything had a drab, dark, menacing quality. She gazed up at the windows with their heavy drapes and wondered if unseen eyes were staring at her from behind them.

Inside, the atmosphere was just as grim and forbidding. They were greeted by a clean-cut looking man of middle age in a gray business suit.

Geoffrey introduced him. "My wife, Enid. This is Francis James, Uncle Ford's business manager."

Francis James had a lean face. His shrewd gray eyes fixed on her as he extended his hand to her. "Delighted to meet you, Enid. We've prepared an apartment for you and Geoffrey, newly decorated. I'm sure we've all looked forward to your coming."

"Thank you," she said. He at once struck her as cold but no doubt extremely capable.

Geoffrey asked him, "Where's Mother?"

"Resting," the lawyer said. "She'll meet your wife at dinner."

"And Peter?"

"Your brother is out walking somewhere," Francis James said with a look of disapproval. "He waited for you awhile then became restless and left the house."

Geoffrey looked slightly disappointed but he turned to her and said, "It doesn't matter. You'll meet them both at dinner."

"Of course," she said.

Francis James gave Geoffrey a sharp glance. "As soon as you have your things settled in your room I wish you'd take a few minutes to go upstairs and see your uncle. He's been very dejected this last week."

"I'll go up as soon as I can," Geoffrey promised.

The lawyer smiled at Enid apologetically. "You'll forgive me for bringing up the matter. But we live under a strain in this house. Mr. Ford Hunt has not enjoyed good health lately."

"That's tragic," she said.

"We feel so," the lawyer agreed. And he told Geoffrey, "We opened two additional rooms next to yours to form the apartment.

I hope you'll like the arrangement."

"Thank you," Geoffrey said.

They left the lawyer and went up the cavernous stairway. Enid found the old mansion like some scary setting for a horror picture. It had the same outlandish style and type of furnishing. Little had been done to change its decor over the years and it would be an almost hopeless task to do so.

Their three-room apartment was on the second floor on the ocean side of the ancient house. Enid was pleasantly surprised by the apartment. It had been painted in bright tones to relieve some of the gloom of the place and the furniture was reasonably modern. She felt that she could live there more comfortably than in the rest of the mansion.

Geoffrey also seemed impressed. "They've done a good job of decorating," he said. "I expect Martha has been brought into this."

"Martha?" she said. It was the first time she'd heard him mention the name. And now he did so with the utmost casualness.

He glanced at her with a smile. "I guess I haven't mentioned her."

"No," she said.

"She's a house guest here, in fact almost a permanent one. She's an artist and this part

26

of the coast interests her. Her father was a good friend of Uncle Ford's. And he long ago gave her permission to live here whenever she liked. At the present her father is on a mission for the State Department in India and they've closed their place down the cliffs for a few months. And she's been living here."

Enid listened to it all with an inner dismay. She said, "I take it this Martha is an old family friend?"

"Yes. Mother is very fond of her," he enthused.

"And you?"

"I've known her through the years. When I came here on summer holidays she and I romped the cliffs together."

Enid gave him a mocking look. "I trust your days of romping together have ended?"

Geoffrey looked embarrassed and blushed violently. "You can be sure of that. She's a nice girl. But we're just good friends now."

"You say your mother likes her. And your famous uncle, Ford Hunt. Did they expect you to marry her?"

"I wouldn't know," Geoffrey said uneasily. "In any case, I didn't."

"No, you didn't," she agreed slowly.

"And I notice that your mother or none of the others were on hand to greet me."

"Don't worry about that!" he protested.

"I'll try not to," she said. "But I can't help wondering how welcome I'm going to be here. Not even your lawyer friend seemed too enthusiastic about my arrival."

"Don't mind Francis — he's a cold type."

"I can see that," she said grimly. Then she gave him a warning look, "You'd better go up and see your uncle at once. I can unpack. After all, that's why we rushed back here so madly."

He hesitated. "You don't mind?"

"Of course not," she said. "I expected you'd have to do it as soon as we got here."

"I'll tell Uncle Ford about you," he promised.

"Thanks," she said. "But I'll be surprised if I get any poem of welcome. I'm beginning to feel like an intruder here."

"You mustn't," he begged, taking her by the arms. "I love you and want you here with me. Nothing else matters." And he touched his lips to hers.

She looked at him ruefully. "I wish you weren't so charming. If you hadn't been, I don't think you'd ever have talked me into this."

"As long as I managed," he said with a

smile and then he left her.

He was gone for a long while. She finished unpacking and stood by the window gazing out at the mist-covered ocean. It was a lonely, dreary place. No doubt it would be much different on a sunny day. But with the fog it was miserable.

She stared at the heavy mist and thought about her husband someplace upstairs in the old mansion talking to Ford Hunt, the eccentric old poet who was his uncle. She tried to picture them together and wondered what they might be saying to each other. Was the famed poet asking about her? Would he break his rule of solitude and come down to see her? Or perhaps invite her up there? Either way she'd feel more welcome in the old house.

She was standing with her back to the door from the hallway and all at once she heard a floorboard creak. She turned fearfully to find herself gazing at a bizarre figure. A short, hunchbacked man with a sallow, long face surmounted by coarse graying hair. His deepset eyes had a fanatic's burning light in them and in his hands he held a rifle!

CHAPTER TWO

Before she could break her shocked silence the man in the shabby black suit introduced himself. "I'm Watts," he said in a low, thin voice. "I'm Ford Hunt's manservant. I'm afraid I have frightened you. I didn't know anyone was in the apartment yet. I came to return Mr. Geoffrey's rifle."

She relaxed slightly. "I'm sorry. I didn't hear you come in until the floorboard creaked. It gave me a start."

"Yes," the hunchbacked Watts nodded his gray head agreeably as if this was quite the expected thing. He said, "I'll just put the rifle in Mr. Geoffrey's closet where it belongs." And he vanished into the adjoining room.

Enid was ashamed that she had shown such surprise. But at any rate Watts had not seemed to be offended by her manner. As he glided back into the room on his way out, she said, "I've heard about you, Watts. And how faithful you have been to Ford Hunt."

The hunchback paused and gave her a strange look. "Thank you," he said quietly.

"Welcome to Cliffcrest."

"I'm sure I'll like it here," she said.

"Mr. Geoffrey is a wonderful young man," Watts said. "I would expect him to make an ideal husband."

"I have no doubts about him," she smiled. "Just the place."

"It's not always as gloomy as this," he said. "The fog accounts for most of the unpleasantness."

"Do you get a lot of it?"

"On this particular point we do," Watts said. "Strangely, just a little to the left or right of us there is usually sunshine most of the time."

"Did Ford Hunt know that when he bought the property?"

The hunchback looked sad. "He was younger then and spent only a small part of his time here. Now he makes it his permanent residence. And he no longer cares much what the weather may be like."

"I see," she said.

The quiet-spoken Watts left her to ponder on this. Gradually, she was coming to the opinion that Ford Hunt might be insane at least part of the time. Apparently this illness dated back to the tragic plunge from the balcony which had taken his young wife's life. Or had she committed suicide?

She recalled the scandal sheets had made some hints otherwise when the young woman's death was still news. Now it had all been forgotten.

Forgotten everywhere but in this old house, she decided. Here the tragedy was a fact which overwhelmed everything. Perhaps it also explained the silent, fearsome atmosphere of the place. And if Ford Hunt, the sensitive old poet, had suffered another breakdown as the result of his loss, they were keeping it from the public. Not an easy thing to do but possible by his remaining in his attic retreat.

What was Geoffrey's role in it all? According to his story he was the one person who could rouse the old poet from his depression and make him go on living and working. It was surely a heavy responsibility for Geoffrey — and yet he wanted to assume it. And she had promised not to interfere with his role in the strange household.

Was it possible that everyone in the house deferred to a madman? For all she knew Ford Hunt might be a raving lunatic? But then she realized this was not possible since he had kept on turning out poetry. It was no secret that Ezra Pound, when mentally upset, had been able to turn out fine poetry. The same thing could be true in the case of Ford Hunt.

In any case, Geoffrey was the only one who seemed to be able to handle the famous poet. It was a weird situation which she would have preferred to avoid. But it was too late to have misgivings now. She had married Geoffrey and that was that!

It was almost an hour and a half before Geoffrey returned to her. By then it was nearing dinner time. The moment he stepped inside the room she was shocked. There was an ashen grayness beneath his tanned skin and a look of weary desperation in his blue eyes. He stared at her a moment in silence.

"How did it go?" she asked.

He took a few steps toward her. "The sessions in the attic are always hard on me."

"Was he angry about your marriage?" she worried.

"He didn't mention it."

She was shocked and a little hurt. "Doesn't he care?"

Geoffrey frowned. "He was very upset about something else."

"Oh?"

"It's a kind of anniversary for him, and these days anniversaries appear to upset him."

"I see," she said. "You seem utterly exhausted."

"I am," he sighed. "I'm sorry I was so long."

"I expected you would be. You've been away quite awhile."

"Yes. That's it."

"Were you able to cheer him up? Help him?"

Geoffrey shrugged. "You never know in his case. He may just sit there in a mood or perhaps tonight he'll begin writing and put down some gem of a poem."

"But at least he talked to you?"

"As much as he ever does," Geoffrey said. Then he gave her a troubled glance. "There's something that perhaps should be understood between us."

Something in his manner made her tense. She felt he might be about to make some awful disclosure. His dejected manner and his reluctance to talk freely about what had happened upstairs was proving frightening to her.

She said in a low voice, "Yes?"

"This business of my uncle. I don't always like to discuss it."

"Why?"

"It's very tiring," he said. "I'll be called up there often. And many times I'll not even know what I've accomplished when I am finished. Ford Hunt is not an easy man to reason with. I come away from him depressed and confused."

"I can understand that," she said.

His weary eyes met hers. "I can't face the prospect of being questioned by you every time I come down from the attic. I can't or won't give you a resume of what has gone on up there every time I'm called to Uncle Ford's side."

"I didn't mean to interfere," she said in a hurt tone.

He waved a hand to placate her. It was a tired gesture. "I know you want to help," he said. "I don't question that. I'm only trying to make the situation clear. Don't badger me about what goes on up there."

"I won't. You only had to explain," she said.

"Explaining isn't easy. I had no right to bring you into this," he said abjectly. "I knew it was a risk. Unfair to you!"

She went to him and put an arm around him. "You're wrong! I don't mind at all. It's just that I didn't understand."

"Well, now you do," he said.

"Yes, now I do," she repeated. And to change the subject she told him, "While you were gone Watts came here with a rifle he said was yours."

Geoffrey frowned. "Yes. I'd let Peter have the rifle. He must have finished with it."

"Watts put it in the closet for you."

"Good."

"He's a strange man. He glided in here so silently I didn't hear him."

Her husband said, "He's been a very faithful servant to my uncle."

"I have no doubt of that," she said.

Geoffrey looked at his watch. "It's time to shower and change and join the others at dinner."

Enid felt a mild panic. "This is going to be my moment of ordeal," she warned him.

"Nonsense," he told her. "You'll manage beautifully."

As it turned out she didn't do all that well. Geoffrey's mother, Gertrude Hunt, presided at the long dinner table in the high-ceilinged paneled dining room. She was a well-preserved woman in her mid-fifties with a square, still-attractive face and an arrogant manner. She greeted Enid with a frozen smile and a few polite words. For the rest of the meal she mostly talked to the others.

The others besides Geoffrey and Enid included lawyer Francis James, who seemed to get along with Geoffrey's mother well.

He was the same aloof, somewhat over-bearing type. Then there was Peter, her husband's younger brother, a hippie-style youth with long brown hair to his shoulders and a thin mustache which didn't enhance a good-looking but basically weak face. The other member of the dinner party was Martha Krail, a black-haired beauty with a cool charm.

Martha was sitting across from Enid and so they managed to talk quite a lot. Enid at once had the impression that the even-featured Martha was clever and maybe still in love with Geoffrey. Every so often she cast admiring glances in Geoffrey's direction.

She told Enid, "You must be very happy."

Enid said, "I think I'll grow to like it here."

"I mean with Geoffrey," Martha said. "I'll make no predictions as to how you'll like this old house."

"But this is a wonderful house," Geoffrey's mother said at once. "And you should know that Martha. You've spent so much of your life here."

The dark girl smiled at Geoffrey's mother. "I wasn't speaking for myself. I think Enid has to decide about Cliffcrest on her own."

"That's reasonable," lawyer Francis James chimed in.

Long-haired Peter Hunt smiled mysteriously at Enid but made no comment. In fact, she realized, he'd said little all during the dinner. But there had been some mocking quality in that smile he hadn't wanted her to miss. She made up her mind to seek him out and try to talk to him at the earliest opportunity.

Geoffrey's mother went on in her arrogant way, "Ford wrote some of his finest poetry after coming here. I'm sure the magnificent view must have inspired him."

"I imagine it is lovely," Enid said. "But it has been foggy since I arrived."

"And it will be much of the time," Martha warned her. "When I want to paint I go further along the coast. It's amazing what a difference a few miles make."

Francis James gave her a politely inquiring look. "Do you have some special talent, Mrs. Hunt?"

Enid shook her head. "No. Just caring for Geoffrey."

"I'd say that was enough," the lawyer smiled thinly.

"I don't agree," Gertrude Hunt said. "I think one should develop some talent or skill. Even if it be frivolous. I had a grandfather, poor old dear, who collected butter-flies. I'm sure it kept him alert and active beyond his years."

Enid said, "I was a secretary. I type well and I'm excellent at dictation. Perhaps in time I could help Mr. Ford Hunt with some of his poetry."

There was a moment of what seemed stunned silence at the table. It was as if she'd dropped some kind of bombshell. The others glanced about them uneasily. No one seemed ready to answer her.

Then Francis James said in his smoothest legal manner, "I fear that would be impossible. The only person Mr. Hunt allows to take down dictation from him is Geoffrey. So it would seem that your husband has spoiled any plans you might have in that direction."

Geoffrey gave her a look which she interpreted as almost a plea for her to be silent. He said, "You needn't worry about it, Enid."

Martha spoke up in the manner of one bravely changing the turn of the conversation, saying, "Do you like to read, Enid?"

"Yes," she said. "I read everything. And I'm fond of poetry. Ford Hunt has always been one of my idols. And beyond poetry I think of him as a truly great American of his time."

Francis James nodded approval. "You are right. And in spite of his living in virtual retirement the public awaits his every new book with eagerness. It is remarkable how his hold on the reading world continues."

Enid said, "It's his marvelous talent. And I think his last book was perhaps his best."

The long-haired Peter Hunt again smiled her way. Perhaps this time a smile of approval. The last book of Ford Hunt's poems had been directed to the hippie generation in an amazing way, considering Ford Hunt's age. No doubt Peter had admired the book.

The conversation changed to a discussion of the latest oil spillage in the area and what the government was doing about it and what they should be doing to clean the situation up. Enid felt unable to offer opinions so she mostly listened. When they left the table she noticed that the attractive Martha at once sought Geoffrey out and walked to a secluded corner of the living room to talk with him.

She found herself with lawyer James for an escort. The austere middle-aged man said, "I expect you find this quite a change — being removed from New York and thrown into the lap of a family in a new section of the country."

Enid managed a smile. "Geoffrey prepared me for it. He told me he worked very closely with his uncle."

The lawyer furrowed his brow as they crossed the foyer to the living room where everyone was gathering. He said, "I wonder if he explained the extent of his association with Ford Hunt. With the old man as ill as he is these days, Geoffrey has to give a major portion of his time to him."

She looked at the lawyer with questioning eyes. "Just how ill is Ford Hunt?"

He looked uneasy. "Not ill in the usual sense of the word. Just old and tired."

"I see."

"Your position here will not be easy," the lawyer warned her. "And yet it is imperative that Geoffrey live here."

"I'll manage somehow," she said.

The lawyer nodded gravely. "May I offer some words of friendly advice?"

"Of course," she said.

"Don't ask too many questions, don't let the atmosphere of this old house frighten you and try to get along with Geoffrey's mother."

She gave him a thin smile. "I may find the last the most difficult."

Francis James sighed. "Gertrude is a difficult — though well meaning — woman. She was widowed early and has been overly possessive of her sons. You may have heard of her trouble with Peter."

"Yes."

"That is still a problem and I believe she had ideas that Martha and Geoffrey might marry. His deciding on you was an upset. Though I'm sure you and he are better suited than he and Martha."

She looked over where Geoffrey and Martha were still in conversation. She said, "They still seem very close."

"And they always will be," the lawyer said. "If you find the going too difficult here my advice is to give it up. Leave Geoffrey and call it a bad job. He'll always have these ties. As long as Ford Hunt lives and stays in the same state of health he is in now, there'll be no ease for Geoffrey. He'll have to go on being his uncle's voice to the world."

Enid listened to the lawyer's cold statement of facts and decided that he was not on her side. He might pretend to be a friend but he was like the others, interested in getting rid of her.

She said, "I'm not ready to give up on the day of my arrival, Mr. James. You ought to at least allow a proper amount of time for me to be discouraged."

Faint tinges of crimson showed on his

thin, gray cheeks. "I'm sorry, Mrs. Hunt. I shouldn't have touched on these matters. It is not my place to interfere." And he turned and walked away from her.

She stood by herself for a few minutes feeling glumly out of it. The lawyer went down to the other end of the room and joined Geoffrey's mother. Enid was about to leave the living room and start upstairs when the long-haired Peter Hunt sidled up to her. The former drug addict gave her another of his cynical smiles.

"How do you like the family?" he asked.

She said, "I hardly know. I've only just gotten here."

Peter Hunt gazed derisively at the four gathered at the other end of the room and told her, "You're not going to make it here."

"Why not?"

Geoffrey's piano-playing brother gave her a knowing glance. "The climate isn't right for you. What made you marry Geoff?"

"I suppose I fell in love with him."

"That's asking for trouble," Peter jeered at her. "Don't you know he's Ford Hunt's puppet? Geoff has no life of his own at all since our dear uncle lost his wife."

"Were you here when she killed herself?"

He shook his head. "I was away. But I've

heard lots about it. Did you know today is the fifth anniversary of her death?"

"No," she said, impressed. "Geoffrey mentioned something about his uncle being in a bad state because it was an anniversary but he didn't say what."

"That's what."

"It must be awful for him to remember," Enid said.

"I'd guess so," the younger Hunt brother said calmly. "Especially since she may not have plunged off that balcony deliberately."

"What do you mean?"

"There are whispers around that the old man became jealous of her and shoved her over the balcony himself."

"Ford Hunt? You don't believe that about him?"

"I've never seen him since I've come back here," the ex-drug addict said. "So I wouldn't know."

"But Ford Hunt is a fine man. A truly great poet," she protested. "I can't think of him murdering his wife."

"Then why has he locked himself up there ever since?"

"I can't imagine. He's very sensitive, I hear. Perhaps because of grief."

"Maybe he's punishing himself," Peter

44

Hunt said laconically. "You ever think of that?"

"I haven't given it any thought," she said.

The young man with the long hair and mustache looked at the high ceiling of the living room. "Doesn't it make you feel sort of odd to know there's someone living up there who never leaves the attic? Never sees anyone but Geoff and Watts. Never speaks to a living soul but those two."

"Genius is often strange," she said. "Your uncle is a genius."

"He may also be dangerously insane," Peter Hunt warned her. "I have the conviction that one day he'll leave that attic and all Hell will break loose."

She shivered. "What a nasty prediction."

His weird eyes met hers. "That's why I say you'll have a bad time here. You should get out before anything really grim happens."

"I think you're exaggerating the dangers."

"Maybe. How do you feel about ghosts?"

"Ghosts?"

He offered her another of his secret smiles. "People claim they see the ghost of Ford Hunt's wife around. Some of the help say they've seen her on the lawn and on the balcony from which she's supposed to have jumped to her death. And Martha claims she ran into her once in the foyer."

"But you've never seen it?" she said.

"No," Peter said, "I've never seen it. But I don't believe in ghosts."

"Neither do I."

"I wish you luck," the young man with the long hair grinned. "I can't talk any longer — I have a date to keep with a piano at a bar."

"Do you work every night?"

"I play in the same bar every night if you call it work," Peter said with a smile. "My mother thinks I'm disgracing her."

"That shouldn't bother you if you're doing something worthwhile that you like."

"It fills in the time," he said. "That's what has always bugged me: time. See you around!" And with a wave of his hand he sauntered out in the direction of the front door.

Enid watched him go with a feeling of bewilderment. It had been a strange evening. The Hunt family were just a bit more than she'd bargained for. It was hard to dislike Peter but it was also hard to decide just what sort of person he was. The fact he'd been on drugs was against him. He clearly was the rebel of the family. Whether she could look on him as a friend or not was doubtful.

Martha and Geoffrey broke up with Martha leaving the room. Geoff came over to her. He said, "I noticed you were talking with Peter."

She gave him a small smile. "You were so engrossed with Martha I doubted you'd notice anything."

"We had a few things to catch up on."

"Evidently."

"Was Peter doing his usual thing of knocking the family?"

She said, "Is that what he regularly does?"

"Yes," Geoffrey said with a scowl. "He's my brother but I can't recommend him as suitable company. He may still be on drugs and he's definitely hostile to the rest of us."

"That seems to be normal with younger brothers."

"Peter goes beyond the normal," Geoffrey said grimly. "Would you like to take a stroll outside? I think the fog may be lifting some."

"If you like," she said.

They went out by the front door and she saw that the fog was still heavy enough. But they went for a stroll along the circular asphalt driveway. When they were a distance from the house she looked back and saw that among the lights showing from Cliffcrest's windows there was a solitary one from the attic floor.

Gazing up at the amber glow through the

blind of the attic window, she asked, "Is that Ford Hunt's study?"

"Yes," her husband said. "He often works there until late in the night."

She gave the handsome Geoff a knowing glance. "Tonight must be especially difficult for him."

He showed surprise. "Why do you say that?"

"You spoke of its being an anniversary."

"Oh, that."

Enid continued to study her husband's face. "And I was told by Peter that it is the anniversary of his wife's suicide."

Geoffrey at once showed anger. "Peter would do better to keep his mouth shut!"

"Is that so?"

"He wasn't even here when Ellen took her life," Geoffrey went on in a rage.

"You haven't told me," she reminded him quietly.

Her husband's bronzed face showed his upset. "Yes it is. Ellen died five years ago tonight."

"And Ford Hunt has never left that attic since?"

"No."

"I find it a very strange story."

"You shouldn't bother yourself with it," Geoffrey said. "My brother shouldn't have mentioned it to you."

"I disagree," she said. "I think I should know all the past history of this place and its people."

"Why burden your brain?"

"For instance," she said, "what about the rumor that Ellen didn't jump to her death but was shoved over the balcony by your uncle?"

He gasped. "Did Peter tell you that?"

"Yes."

"I can understand strangers dealing in that filthy type of rumor," Geoffrey raged. "But I can't forgive Peter for it. And especially not when he retells the story to you!"

"Why did the rumor start?"

"How do any of them start? My uncle is a famous man. People enjoy telling stories about famous men. Trying to blacken their characters."

"I take it you don't believe the rumor."

"No!"

"You're very emphatic," she said. "I don't suppose you've ever seen Ellen's ghost either? They claim her unhappy spirit roams here on certain nights."

Her husband looked grim. "No. I have not seen the ghost."

"I believe Martha has."

"Martha saw a shadow one night," he said disgustedly. "And she at once decided it had been a ghost."

"I must talk to her about it."

"You're coming here with the wrong attitude," Geoffrey warned her. "You should try to enjoy the old house not dream up a lot of horrible things about it."

"I don't mean to."

"Then forget about all that nonsense," he said as they stood in the fog-laden driveway together. "I tried to explain before we came here. I told you it wouldn't be easy."

She had been watching that upstairs window as he talked. And she saw the shadow of a head and shoulders appear against the blind and then move away.

"I think I just saw him!" she exclaimed.

"Who?"

"Your uncle, Ford Hunt," she said. "He came and stood before the blind for a moment just now."

"It must be Watts you saw!"

"Why?" she turned to him in surprise. "Why couldn't it have been your uncle?"

Geoffrey looked baffled. He flustered, "I don't say it wasn't but the chances are all against it. When he is working he rarely leaves his desk. And at this time of night Watts goes up to get his bed ready and make the place tidy."

"You and Watts have keys to the attic?"

"Yes. We're the only ones. When I was away Watts had the sole contact with my uncle. That was why I had to rush back. It was getting near the anniversary of Ellen's death and he was becoming extremely depressed."

"Have you been able to help him?"

"I hope so," he said. "It's too soon to tell yet."

They strolled on a little further. She'd not been satisfied with all the answers her husband had given her concerning the death of Ellen and the supposed appearances of her ghost. She had the uneasy feeling that he was holding something back from her. He had no wish for her to know all the facts.

Reaching the edge of the cliff they were able to look down and see the foam as the waves dashed in against the jagged rocks. Cliffcrest had been built so that one section of it was directly above the beach. It was from one of the end balconies just five years ago that very night that the beautiful Ellen had either jumped or been pushed from the balcony.

She turned to try and decide which balcony the girl had been on when she'd toppled to her death. She supposed it would be the third floor. And as she searched the balconies on the third level overlooking the ocean she suddenly gave a startled cry. For on the end balcony nearest them clearly outlined against the gray mist was the figure of a woman with hands outstretched!

CHAPTER THREE

Geoffrey heard her startled cry and turned to her. "What's wrong?"

"Look, up there!" she exclaimed, pointing to the balcony.

"What?" he asked blankly.

"A figure," she told him. And even as she spoke she knew she'd not a hope of backing up her statement. The shrouded female figure had quickly vanished. But she went on, "I saw a girl on that end balcony!"

"You have to be joking!" he protested.

She gave him a searching look. "That is the one, isn't it?"

"You're talking in riddles," he shot back. "What one?"

"The balcony," she said excitedly. "It is the same balcony from which Ellen fell to her death?"

He hesitated, "What if it is?"

"Just tell me!"

"All right," her husband said in a weary voice. "It was the end balcony. Now I suppose you want to make me admit you saw her ghost on it?"

"I saw something," she said triumphantly.

"I can't stop you from being scared by shadows," Geoffrey said with some impatience.

"But this wasn't a shadow. I saw her clearly."

Geoffrey shook his head. "You see what comes of Peter's tall tales. People like you start believing them."

"But I did see something!"

"I doubt that very much," her husband said. But he added, "Let's go on inside."

She was still thinking about the ghostly creature she'd just seen on the balcony. "What about that room?" she asked her husband.

"What about it?"

"Is it kept locked?"

"Yes," he said. "It's not in use any longer. At my uncle's request we keep it continually locked."

"I thought so!"

"Why?"

"It means it couldn't have been anyone in the house who went out there," she pointed out to him. "It had to be a phantom."

Geoffrey said disgustedly, "That doesn't prove anything. What you saw was an illusion!"

"Perhaps," she said quietly as they entered the old house again. But she didn't believe it. She was certain she had seen the ghost of the famous poet's wife.

In their own apartment, just before they went to bed, she asked Geoffrey, "What went on at the time of Ellen's death?"

In pajamas he hesitated by the bed to give her an irritated look. "Make your question a bit more clear!"

She was in bed with her knees up under the coverings and her hands clasped around them. "Where were you when she went over the balcony?"

He frowned. "Downstairs in the study. Why?"

"Did you hear her scream?"

"Yes."

"What did you do?"

"I didn't know what it was at first," Geoffrey recalled. "Then I heard running footsteps coming down the corridor and Watts came and told me there'd been a dreadful accident."

"And then what?"

"I went out and found her broken body."

"Where were the others?"

"I don't exactly remember," he said. "They turned up later."

"You must know," she insisted. "There

had to be an investigation. They must have given testimony."

He sat heavily on the side of the bed and ran his hand across his brow in a tired gesture. "I guess mother was in her room and Francis James was out for a midnight walk. Neither Martha nor Peter were here at the time."

"Did your mother and Francis James join you soon after you found the body?"

He nodded. "They were there before Watts was able to cover the body with a blanket and we all waited for the police to arrive."

She asked the question which had been bothering her. "And where was Ellen's husband during all this? Where was Ford Hunt?"

Geoffrey gave her a grim glance. "Still upstairs."

"Surely he had heard her?"

"He was in the room with her before she ran to the balcony and jumped to her death," he said. "The shock of it sent him into a kind of weird mental state. We went upstairs to find him seated in an easy chair with an open book on his lap."

"He had a mental collapse," she suggested.

"A brief one," Geoffrey admitted. "He came out of it by the time the police arrived.

He was able to answer their questions."

"Did he tell why she did it?"

"It had been building up. He was jealous of her. There had been many quarrels," Geoffrey said.

"And it was after that he began his solitary existence in the attic?"

"Yes. A few days later he went up there and set up a headquarters. He's never left it since."

"Hardly the act of a sane man," she ventured.

Geoffrey frowned. "I don't say that he is completely sane but he's not mad either. At any rate we can be thankful he has retained his ability to write."

"As long as he produces his poetry you think there's nothing to worry about," she said.

He looked surprised. "Meaning what?"

"Meaning he might become a dangerous lunatic and threaten your life when you go up there to help him. He could threaten all the lives under this roof and more."

"There's no danger."

"You sound so sure."

"I am," her husband said. "After all I see him more often than anyone else."

"I can't argue with you there," she admitted.

He looked at her earnestly. "Why should you be so concerned with a girl who died five years ago? Someone you never met? Whom you know nothing about! You should forget her!"

"I find that hard to do," she said, glancing about the shadowed room. "Perhaps it's this house. It holds something of her. It could be the ghost I saw tonight is here unseen urging me on to ask these questions."

Her handsome young husband looked startled. "You mustn't allow yourself such morbid thoughts."

"You asked for an explanation. I'm trying to give you one," she said.

"Let's drop it for tonight," he said, reaching to turn out the one remaining light.

But long after he'd gone to sleep the vision of that phantom on the balcony tormented her. She knew that in coming to Cliffcrest she had involved herself in that unsolved mystery of years ago. She didn't quite understand how but she felt she was meant to play a part in its unravelling and that it could be that a ghostly presence would help her do it.

The regular crash of the waves on the beach helped her find sleep. And for a while she slept and dreamed of being with Geoffrey. They were standing on the cliffs, hand in hand, staring down at a small offshore island with an interesting pattern of trees on it. Suddenly she screamed as she sensed some shapeless threat bear down upon her. She couldn't make out what it was as she fell under its attack.

There was the weird sensation of falling and then she woke up in a welter of perspiration. At her side Geoffrey still slept on. She didn't want to wake him and yet she was in a frantic state as the result of her dream. It had been as vivid as if it had really happened.

Gently she slid from the large double bed she was occupying with her husband and put on her slippers. Then she crossed the room to the window and looked out. The fog was still thick. She wondered how long it could last. As she was standing by the window she thought she heard footsteps from the corridor outside their door.

The footsteps advanced to just outside the door and then began to retreat. Her curiosity taking control of her she went to the door and gently edged it open in an effort to see who it was had passed by their door. Staring into the darkness of the hallway she was unable to see anything.

Opening the door a bit more she moved out into the hallway itself and still wasn't able to see anything. She turned to go back inside and then suddenly stiffened and stood still.

From down at the end of the hallway she heard her name in a ghostly whisper. "Enid!"

A chilling horror raced through her and she was unable to speak or move. And then again in the same hoarse whisper she was able to clearly distinguish her name.

"Enid!" the phantom whispered plaintively. "Enid!"

Then she managed to turn and stare into the shadows from whence the sound had come. And there was no one to be seen. She hadn't thought there would be. She quickly went on inside and shut the door and then leaned against it weakly. She could still hear the macabre whispering of the voice in her imagination.

When she had regained some control of herself she crept softly back to bed and got in without waking Geoffrey. What did it mean? Had she truly heard a ghost? Or had the near-mad poet come down in the after-midnight quiet to roam the old house? Had he known her name and whispered it to her in the darkness? She couldn't make up her mind.

She knew that Geoffrey would only scoff if she told him about it. So she decided to keep it to herself until a suitable moment. In the meantime she'd not soon forget it. Nor would she forget her dream! What had it meant? And what had been the sudden threat which had come to her on the cliffs? She was speculating on these questions when she fell asleep.

With the morning came warm sunshine. She was hardly able to believe it when she got up. Geoffrey was shaved and dressed and already downstairs. She went to the window and took a look out at the ocean revealed now that the fog had gone out. It was a truly lovely view from the old house and made her realize why the poet had bought it.

Enid took a leisurely shower, put on a favorite vivid yellow pants suit and went downstairs. At the breakfast table she found Geoffrey and his mother. The older woman inclined her head in a nod of greeting.

"Did you sleep well your first night at Cliffcrest?" her mother-in-law asked.

She managed a small smile. "It seems I overslept. I'm the last one down to breakfast."

"No," Gertrude Hunt said with a grim look on her strong-featured face. "Peter has not come down. But he seldom has any breakfast."

Geoffrey spoke above his grapefruit. "We take things in an easy stride here. You can come down at any hour you like. Please feel that."

"Thanks," she said, tackling her own grapefruit. "It's better than racing for the subway on a deadline."

"You said you were a secretary in New York," the older woman said.

"She had a top secretarial job," Geoffrey interrupted. "Her boss allowed her to buy art objects for him. That's where we first met — at a gallery on Madison Avenue."

His mother glared at him. "Will you kindly allow me to talk to your wife without your interjecting comments?"

"I was only trying to explain," he said unhappily and returned to giving his attention to the grapefruit.

"I had a good position," Enid said. "You might call it one of trust. I handled large amounts of money for my employer and he used me as a go-between in some important transactions."

The older woman eyed her coldly. "I'm afraid you're going to find it dull here."

"I'm sure I'll enjoy it," she insisted.

"We have a lot of land," her husband said. "You can stroll around the beaches and in the fields. You won't feel shut in as you do in the city."

"We have extensive grounds," Gertrude Hunt agreed. "But Geoffrey ought to have warned you that we are rather isolated. Quite a distance from the nearest estate."

"I assumed that on the long drive in," she said.

"It has its disadvantages," her mother-in-law warned. "Especially in these days of hippies and drug takers. We get a certain number of transients. Some of them have the nerve to sleep on the beach within sight of this house. I've seen their sleeping bags down there."

"Most of them are harmless, Mother," Geoffrey remonstrated.

"I'm glad you said most of them," his mother said in her cold acid fashion. "For one of our girls was attacked about ten days ago by one of them."

"Was she badly hurt?" Geoffrey asked. "This happened when I was in New York."

"That — along with a lot of other things," Gertrude Hunt told him. "She was bruised and scratched but her screams attracted the gardener who came to her rescue. Both he and she claimed her attacker was a monstrous-looking tramp in ragged clothing who fled toward the shore."

"That's an isolated case," Geoffrey

argued. "It might not happen again for ages."

"I should hope not," his mother said sternly. "But only a night or two ago the housekeeper looked out her window and saw the same dreadful-looking tramp, so it seems he's still lurking around the estate."

"The housekeeper might have imagined she saw someone," Geoffrey said. "Once a story like that gets going people keep repeating it."

"I don't think that is true in this case," his mother told him. "Mrs. Blossom is not given to wild imaginings."

Enid said little but listened to the exchange between her husband and his mother with a good deal of interest. She was thinking of her own weird experiences since her arrival at the old mansion. The memory of the phantom figure on the balcony and the eerie voice calling her name in the corridor were still vivid. And the nightmare she'd had of some crushing danger on the cliffs also remained clear in her mind.

Geoffrey's mother left the breakfast table first and this gave Enid a little time alone with her husband before they began the day.

He asked her, "Have you any plans?"

"Not really," she said.

"I'll be upstairs with Uncle Ford most of

the morning and maybe even part of the afternoon," he told her. "So you'll be left on your own."

She smiled across the table at him. "I'll find plenty to occupy myself. Just familiarizing myself with this lovely old house can keep me busy for awhile."

"It's a fine day," he said. "You should get out of the house as much as you can."

"I will."

He sighed as he pushed his napkin aside on the table. "I'm sorry about this business of Uncle Ford but I have been away for a long while. There's a lot to be caught up."

"Of course," she agreed.

When they parted in the foyer he gave her a husbandly kiss on the cheek before going up the stairs. She watched him go with a kind of sinking feeling. Despite her assurances that she understood that his duties with the famed poet came first, she was going to miss him. What made it particularly difficult being on her own was the impression she had that she was not a welcome addition to the household. For some reason, the tight little group resented her.

She went outside and strolled across the broad lawns fronting on the cliffs. In the bright sunshine the massive green house with its mansarded top story looked less gloomy. Yet it was an ugly structure and nothing could change that. She studied the windows of the attic level where the poet, Ford Hunt, lived his weird hermit existence but could see no signs of life up there.

Reaching the edge of the cliff she stared down at the beach where her mother-in-law contended the hippies were sleeping. Surely there were no signs of them at this moment. She was standing taking in the breathtaking view of ocean and shore when she heard someone coming up behind her. She turned to see the dark-haired Martha in a chic outfit of suede hotpants, cream blouse open at the neck and open jacket with fringed decoration.

Martha smiled as she joined her. "I saw you coming this way."

"A lovely day, isn't it?"

"Perfect," the other girl said. "I'm going down the coast to do some sketching. Would you care to join me? I generally take a lunch and stay a few hours."

It seemed a welcome opportunity to get away from the house and have company. Enid said, "I'd love to go."

"Fine," Martha said. "I'll be leaving in about fifteen minutes and I'll make sure there's lunch enough for two. We'll drive in my jeep."

Enid walked back to Cliffcrest with the other girl and went up and changed into a more casual sports outfit of blue jeans and white sweater. When she went back down Martha was already in the jeep at the front entrance of the old mansion.

Enid got in beside the dark girl. "It's very good of you to ask me along. I'm still awkward here."

Martha smiled as she headed the jeep out of the driveway and along the private road which led to the main highway. "I know how it must be. And this gives us a chance to become better acquainted."

She said, "You're like one of the family."

"I have spent a lot of time here," Martha acknowledged.

"Did you meet Ford Hunt before he became such a recluse?"

"Yes," Martha said. "He used to take me on his knee and recite nonsense poetry to me when I was a little girl. He was a much different person then from what he came to be."

"You weren't here when his wife met her death?"

"No. But I came back for a few days just afterwards. I saw him when the police came to talk to him once. He looked like a ghost of himself, frail and his hair gone completely white."

"Did you know his second wife?"

"Ellen?" Martha said with a hint of bitterness in her tone. "Yes. She was a strange person. Has Geoffrey told you about her?"

"No."

"Then it's a long story. Ellen was never the right sort to marry Ford Hunt. She was a lot younger and very high-strung. But she was one of those people who chase celebrities and Ford Hunt is perhaps America's most celebrated poet."

"Without a doubt."

"So Ellen pursued him until she won his attention. Then she told him she wanted to dedicate her life to him. He was flattered and maybe believed her. Anyway they were married — to the consternation of Gertrude. It was a rocky marriage from the first. I think Ford Hunt felt he was failing in his powers as a poet and he decided to blame her. She wanted him to travel and party and he refused. It was one quarrel after another with them."

"I heard that," Enid said.

Martha shrugged. "Geoffrey's mother didn't make things any easier as you can imagine. She grimly held on to her position as mistress of Cliffcrest and Ellen was caught up in the general stress."

They were still driving along the narrow

private road with its rich greenery on either side. "Then you think that is why she finally took her life."

"I expected something to happen long before it actually did," was Martha's reply.

"You do think she was a suicide?"

Martha glanced quickly from the wheel. "You've heard other stories?"

She said, "I guess there has been talk. Rumors that Ford Hunt was responsible for her death."

"That he pushed her over the balcony during one of their many quarrels?" Martha said.

"Yes."

"I've heard that too," Martha said. "I don't believe it. Ford Hunt wasn't that sort of man. Can you imagine him being able to murder? All his poetry has preached against violence."

Enid frowned. "Only if he'd become insane."

"What has Geoffrey told you about his uncle?"

"Very little. Except that he insists on complete privacy and he depends on Geoffrey to turn his writing over to his publishers."

"Geoffrey has never hinted that his uncle could be mad?"

"No."

"Then I'd accept what Geoffrey has told you," was Martha's advice. "He is closer to Ford Hunt than anyone else with the exception of Watts, his personal servant."

They reached the main highway and drove along its broad surface to a point off the coast about seven miles distant from Cliffcrest. There Martha took a side road that led directly out onto a promontory high above the ocean. It was wide enough for her to drive the jeep close to its edge. Below, there was an almost sheer drop of a couple of hundred feet and the view of rocks and waves was outstanding.

Martha parked the jeep and they got out to enjoy the scenery. Then she set up her easel and began to sketch a seascape as Enid sat at her side and talked. It was a pleasant, lazy atmosphere under the warm sunlight and Enid found herself much more at ease.

She even ventured to bring up the matter of her marrying Geoffrey. She said, "I have the feeling that everyone here expected you and Geoffrey would marry. And when I arrived as his wife it was a surprise."

Martha smiled as she worked at the sketch. "You know what people are like. They take far too much for granted. I've always been fond of Geoffrey but he's been more a brother to me than anyone I thought of marrying."

"I'm glad," she said. "I'm pleased that you weren't hurt by what happened."

"I won't say that Geoffrey and I wouldn't have married if no one else had come along," Martha told her frankly. "But in that case I'd feel it would have been a marriage of convenience rather than a true love affair as yours and his undoubtedly must have been."

"I do love him very much," Enid agreed.

"Geoffrey has quality," Martha said in a quiet voice. "You're very lucky."

"What about Peter?"

Martha hesitated in her sketching. "Peter is Geoffrey without balance. He has charm and he's misused it. You know about his drug problems and that he's playing piano in a cheap roadside lounge."

"Yes. He seems to enjoy shocking people. He was the one who first told me that Ellen mightn't have been a suicide."

"That sounds like him."

"And he stressed that her ghost appears at Cliffcrest."

Martha's pretty face shadowed. "He could be right about that."

Enid stared up at the other girl earnestly. "Geoffrey says that you thought you saw the ghost one night. But he claims it was a shadow and your imagination."

The dark girl smiled wryly. "That's an easy way to explain something that bothers you."

"Then you don't agree?"

"I'm afraid not."

"What did you see?"

Martha stared off at the distant silver of the ocean. "It's not anything I like to remember. I was going into the house late one night and suddenly I noticed this figure standing in the shadows of the foyer to the left of me."

"And?"

"I halted. I was terrified. I spoke and asked who it was. But there was no reply. Then the figure moved and came a little closer to me and I was able to make out the pale face of Ellen. She was wearing a kind of cape with a hood. I'd seen her in it on rainy days. Her lips moved as if she were trying to tell me something and her eyes were infinitely sad. Then she vanished as quickly as she had appeared."

Even in the bright sunshine it was an eerie story that sent a chill through Enid. She gave the other girl a frightened look. "It's a terrifying story," she said.

"It happened," Martha said simply.

"So you believe in Ellen's ghost?"

"I must after that experience."

Enid sighed. "Of course Geoffrey wouldn't believe you."

"No. He scoffed at it. But I know what I saw."

Enid said, "I saw something last night. And later I heard something. But I'm sure Geoffrey and the others would only say it was my nerves."

Martha showed interest. "Tell me."

And so Enid told her about the phantom on the balcony and the voice in the corridor that whispered her name. Martha listened attentively and when she finished gave a deep sigh.

Enid asked, "What do you think?"

"I think it was Ellen," the dark girl said. "Did you discuss this with Geoffrey?"

"I mentioned the figure on the balcony but he missed it and so didn't believe me."

"That's to be expected."

"But I agree with you," Enid said. "I'm sure it was the ghost."

Martha said, "You've barely arrived at Cliffcrest and see how deeply involved you are."

"The old house frightens me. You wonder how many ugly secrets it may hide! What it has done to Ford Hunt!"

The dark girl returned to her sketching. "If you're going to be a help to Geoffrey you must put aside your fears."

"I'm afraid that won't be easy," she said.

Martha went on working. Then there was a pause for lunch. Enid felt she knew the girl much better and yet there was a complexity to Martha's nature which she wasn't sure she understood. By mid-afternoon the sun had changed position and the dark girl was weary of painting. She packed her things in the jeep and began the preparations to leave.

Enid stood by the cliff's edge for a final look at the view and to guide Martha as she drove away from the somewhat precarious parking place. She wondered that the dark girl had driven out so far. Martha got in behind the wheel and started the jeep's engine. And then an unexpected and terrifying thing happened. The jeep backed up suddenly instead of going ahead as Enid expected and she found herself caught in its path!

She screamed as she was knocked down and in a blinding flash she recalled her dream of being at the cliff's edge when a strange force bore down on her. This was it!

CHAPTER FOUR

Enid rolled to escape the wheels of the jeep and came to the very edge of the cliff. She clung there precariously for a moment and then the vehicle moved forward properly. Seconds later Martha jumped out from behind the wheel and came running toward her.

"Are you hurt?" the dark girl asked, bending over her in a panic.

She got to her feet and saw that her jeans were torn at one knee. Otherwise she seemed all right. She said, "I think not."

"I don't know what got into me," Martha lamented. "I put the car in reverse when I meant to go ahead."

Enid brushed herself off. "You changed your direction just in time."

"I might have killed you and then myself. A foot more and I'd have backed over the cliff."

"No harm done," she said, though now she saw that her arm had a long scratch on it as well as a bruise.

"I'll never forgive myself," the other girl said.

"Don't think about it anymore," Enid told her.

After a few minutes they both got in the car and began the drive back to Cliffcrest. It wasn't until they were on their way along the highway and she became conscious of Martha's tense and quiet state that she began to wonder about the accident. She glanced at the girl behind the wheel and wondered if she'd deliberately driven the jeep in reverse in an attempt to kill her. It would have seemed an accident and there likely would have been few questions asked.

Though she was shocked at the possibility, Enid could not dismiss it from her mind. She began to think that Martha's calm acceptance of her as Geoffrey's wife might be a facade to dismiss her suspicions. Perhaps Martha was madly in love with Geoffrey and ready to get rid of her at any cost. And no doubt the others in the family would be glad to help her. It was a frightening thought.

As they neared Cliffcrest Martha gave her a nervous glance. She asked, "Would you mind very much if I asked you as a favor not to mention my near accident to anyone here?"

Enid stared at the other girl. "If that's what you want."

"I'd appreciate it," Martha said. "They'd only make a great fuss about it and do no good."

"Very well," she said quietly. She was wondering if the other girl had some underhand reason for wanting this silence from her. It was dreadful to be speculating in this manner but she couldn't help it.

"Especially don't mention it to Geoffrey," Martha went on. "He's the worst of all. And if he knew I'd almost ran over you he'd never allow you to go anywhere with me again."

"You think he'd react that strongly?"

"I'm positive of it," the girl at the wheel said. "You have no idea how uptight he can get. And this would be sure to bother him."

"I suppose so," she agreed reluctantly.

"I'm not going to say anything and if you remain silent there'll be no talk at all. Your jeans aren't torn all that much anyone will notice them."

So it was settled before they left the jeep. Enid debated the girl's motive but didn't much care whether the nasty business was mentioned or not. She would have liked to discuss it with her husband and get his reaction but under the circumstances she would have to go along with Martha's request.

She went directly up to her room and took

a hot bath. It was good to luxuriate in the tub and she felt it would also be of value in easing her several cuts and bruises. She would have to have some simple explanation, like a tumble on the rocks, should Geoffrey notice them and ask some questions.

It wasn't until she was dressing that it came to her with shocking impact why Martha probably wanted her silence. The dark girl had failed in this "accident" designed to kill her and didn't want it mentioned so that it would be linked with a probable planned second attempt. It suggested that the backing of the car had been deliberate and Martha might well try something like it again.

She dressed for dinner and tried to calm her fears by telling herself she was wrong about the artist. But the suspicion continued to lurk in her mind. It gave a new dimension to her terror of the old house and its people.

Geoffrey arrived in their room just as she finished her make-up. When she turned to him she was startled by the look of dejection and weariness on his handsome face. She at once went over to him.

"You look exhausted," she said.

He sighed. "Another difficult day. The

old man is a perfectionist. Often I fail him."

"Tell me about it," she encouraged him, thinking it would ease his mind.

He gave her a troubled glance. "I can't do that! It's against his wishes! You should know that!" And he left her to go over to the easy chair and slump into it.

"I'm sorry," she said.

"It's all right," he said grimly. "I shouldn't be worrying you about such things anyway."

"Of course you should," she protested, going to him and kneeling by his chair. "I have a right to share your burdens."

"This is a rather special one."

"It must be," she worried. "I can only say being at home has changed you completely. You weren't like this in New York when we met."

He eyed her strangely. "I suppose not."

"You were a different person."

"I felt very different," he acknowledged. He gave her a sad look. "Enid, I may have done you a great wrong by marrying you."

"Don't talk like that!"

"I mean it," he said, taking her hand in his. "It was selfish of me. I'm so deeply involved in Uncle Ford's affairs that I haven't any time for a normal life."

"You could tell him it's too much and let

him find someone else," she suggested.

Geoffrey sat up in his chair, shaken by the idea. "No! I couldn't think of that," he said. "He'd not be able to work with anyone else. I must carry on for his sake."

"Is it right if it costs you your health?" she wanted to know.

"I'll manage," her husband said. "It's just that I worry about you. And how you're making out when I'm up there with him."

"It is difficult."

"That's what worries me more than anything else."

"Why not take me up to meet him? I might be able to win him over and do some of the work he normally assigns to you. We could divide the work load and have more time for each other."

"He'd never hear of it," he said disconsolately. "If I took you up there he'd vanish into another room and refuse to meet you."

"But that would be utter rudeness unless he had some good excuse," she said indignantly.

"He has one. He's not normal since Ellen's death. He's simply not able to face people."

"So there's no easy way out," she said.

"Not that I can think of," Geoffrey said. "What about your day? What did you do?"

She told him about her excursion with Martha and carefully omitted any mention of the near accident, though it worried her to keep silent on it.

She said, "It filled in most of the day."

"Sounds interesting," he agreed. "Martha is clever at her painting. She's done some very good work."

"I know."

He gave her an inquiring look. "How do you like her as a person?"

"Nice enough, I guess," she said. "I really don't know her well yet."

"That's so," he said rising. "It looks as if you two are getting off to a good start. I hope so. Martha doesn't get on with everyone. And I wasn't sure how she'd feel about you."

Enid couldn't resist saying, "Because she might have thought she'd be your bride rather than I?"

Geoffrey looked guilty. "We've been over that ground before."

"Not too thoroughly."

"Thoroughly enough," he said in a firm voice. "I wish you wouldn't bring it up again."

"The facts remain," she told him.

"You're wrong," he said. "I never made a promise to Martha."

"Sometimes promises are indicated rather than said plainly."

He frowned. "Not true in this case." And he left her to take a shower.

Dinner was much a repetition of the previous night. After it was over she strolled outside as it was still pleasant. She'd seen the hunchback, Watts, mounting the stairs with a covered tray in his hands as she'd left the house. The ugly little man had nodded to her in his furtive way. She had the impression that he was also feeling the strain of dealing with the near-mad poet.

When she'd read Ford Hunt's poetry she'd always been left with an impression that life was good. And the battle for existence was clearly indicated as a worthy struggle in all his poems. It was depressing to be behind the scenes and know that his life in no way followed the optimistic note of his work. He had allowed his tragedy to crush him and leave him a broken creature difficult to deal with.

It made her question whether her husband's devotion and sacrifice were worthwhile. Perhaps the world should be allowed to know the state the celebrated poet was in. But that might hurt his past good work and so would not be justified. And fine poetry was issuing from that shattered mind in the isolated attic with Geoffrey's help.

How long would the state of things continue? Geoffrey gave her no encouragement that it would be over soon. So it was a problem she might have to live with for a long while. Added to that was the antagonism of her mother-in-law and the family lawyer. She didn't know what to think about Peter, Geoff's brother. He could be either friend or foe. But she was going to be wary of Martha after the close call she'd had on the cliff.

Standing alone on the lawn she stared back at Cliffcrest. She supposed that Watts would be up in the attic now, serving the old poet from the tray she'd seen him carrying. But none of the blinds had been raised. The old man must prefer his living quarters to remain in shade. She was debating on this when she saw the long-haired Peter walking across the lawn to join her. She prepared herself for a difficult few moments since he seemed to enjoy taunting her and asking her questions for which she had no answer.

Coming up to her, he said, "You seem to be a loner?"

"Not really."

"You'll have to learn to be one here."

"So it seems."

He glanced back at the house derisively.

"Can you imagine anyone building a monstrosity like that in this beautiful spot?"

"It's attractive on the inside."

"Moldy! Rotten with the establishment glitter of another age!"

She smiled. "You have special tastes."

"Granted," Geoff's hippie brother said. "And no patience with what Cliffcrest represents."

"Then why do you live here?"

"I remain as an observer."

"Still it is your home," she said.

"Ford Hunt's home," Peter said with a look of disgust. "He adopted us all after my father's death. Of course mother was delighted. It suited her to preside over the household of America's beloved poet!"

"You don't approve of his poetry?"

"A fake!" Peter snapped. "Just as much a fake as he is. A kind of treacle for the masses! Totally indigestible for any mind over ten!"

"That's a pretty awful indictment," she said. "You sound as if you hate Ford Hunt."

"I hate what he stands for."

"I think his poems are excellent. He won the Pulitzer Prize."

"Establishment rites! I'm not interested!"

She raised her eyebrows. "You're a very violent young man."

He shook his head. "You have the wrong brother."

"What do you mean by that?"

Peter's smile wasn't pleasant. "You don't know this new husband of yours very well, do you?"

Enid felt some anger. "Why do you say such a thing?"

"It's true."

"You hate Geoffrey, don't you?" she challenged him.

"Probably. I've never carefully sorted out my feelings. I'm sure they're hostile."

Her eyes flashed with annoyance. "And you'd like our marriage to be a failure!"

"I have no control over that. It depends on you and Geoff, wouldn't you say?"

"I would," she said. "So why do you try to upset me by saying dreadful things about Geoffrey?"

Peter looked amused. "Because I'm telling you the truth. I said he was more violent than I am. And it is true. You've heard all the scandal about me by this time. That I was on dope and may still be hitting it. Let me remind you that drug people are the quiet, withdrawn ones. We don't tend to violence. But a person of Geoffrey's type does."

"Geoffrey is sacrificing himself to help

Ford Hunt continue a dignified and honorable career. What are you doing for your uncle?"

"Not a thing," Peter was quick to reply. "But have you ever asked Geoffrey why he is making this noble sacrifice?"

"I don't need to."

"I disagree," Peter said. "And I know more about it than you do."

The insinuation in his voice troubled her. She said, "What are you hinting?"

"Ask Geoffrey about Ellen."

She stared at the hippie with his scornful smiling face. "What would Geoffrey have to tell me about his uncle's dead wife?"

"Perhaps a good deal. They were close friends you know."

There could be no missing it. Peter was accusing his brother and his uncle's wife of having an affair. She was shocked and frightened at the same time. Could that have been the reason for the bitter quarrels between the poet and his young wife? Had Geoffrey been the reason for her suicide and was that why he was doing penance by devoting himself to the stricken old man?

She said, "What if they were friends?" It was a bluff on her part. To get out of an awkward situation. But the insinuation would continue to haunt her.

"I think Geoff feels a certain amount of guilt in her death," Peter said.

"I doubt it."

"You can't possibly know anything about it. I do," the young man said smugly. "So don't picture Geoff as a saint to me. I won't buy it." And with another of his sneering smiles he turned and began walking slowly back towards Cliffcrest.

She remained where she was, watching his retreat with angry eyes. She had known nothing pleasant would come of their meeting but she'd not been prepared for a bombshell of an accusation such as he'd made. It could signify anything. It could mean that Ellen had thrown herself to her death because of a hopeless love for Geoffrey, or even that Geoffrey had forced her over the balcony rail in a quarrel. Peter had stressed that Geoffrey was a violent man. Was that what he meant?

It didn't seem possible that she should find herself in this nightmare situation. Only a week ago she'd been a happy young bride with a wholly admirable husband. She'd not set eyes on the ugly Cliffcrest or its equally unpleasant people. She'd never heard of the dead Ellen or guessed that the celebrated Ford Hunt was a pathetic, broken recluse. Now she knew all these things and still didn't know what to make of them.

She retraced her steps but instead of going directly into the house she went around to a section of the garden at one end of the mansion. It had rose bushes and hedges and marble seats set out at intervals along its pathways. As she entered the area she came upon Geoffrey and the urbane lawyer, Francis James, talking in serious undertones.

Seeing her, the lawyer at once ceased talking and offered her a smile. "You see it isn't always foggy here, Mrs. Hunt."

"This is a lovely evening," she said.

"You'll have many of them here," the lawyer assured her. He gave her a searching look. "Are you feeling more comfortable in the old house?"

"I think so," she said.

Geoffrey smiled. "It's a change of area as well as a change of house. Enid never lived on the Pacific Coast before."

"This is a most desirable spot," Francis James said. "It is unfortunate Geoffrey has so little time to give you."

"Yes, it is," she said frankly.

The lawyer cleared his throat. "Perhaps it will help if I explain. There are very large stakes at risk here. You may not properly understand that."

"I don't," she said.

"Not until Ford Hunt received the Pulitzer Prize did he get his due recognition."

"But his name has always been known," Enid pointed out.

Francis James showed a thin smile on his gray face. "There is no question of that. He had always had honors galore. But for most of his life the financial returns from his poetry were slim. This house, for instance, and the property surrounding it were purchased with inherited money."

"I didn't realize," she said.

Geoffrey smiled at her. "You thought your husband came from a wealthy family."

"I didn't think about it at all," she confessed.

Her young husband seemed pleased by her reply. "The Hunts have always had some money. We were never poor. But it was old money and getting a little scarce until Uncle Ford became so popular."

The lawyer nodded. "Huge financial success came for Ford Hunt only after the tragedy which robbed him of his wife. It is one of those bitter ironies."

"How sad for him," Enid said.

"And for his estate if Geoffrey had not been able to step in at the time of his uncle's near-collapse and help guide him back to a working state. The books which have brought a flow of money and recognition to Ford Hunt have been the four volumes which have come out in the past five years."

"I see," she said.

"They have been more relevant to today's people and problems in a surprising way," the lawyer went on. "I have negotiated several of them for the words of popular ballads, a thing we never did before. If Ford Hunt can go on producing poetry of the quality he's doing now for even another five years he should win himself many new honors and leave an extremely large estate."

Enid glanced up toward the attic of Cliffcrest. "Do you feel he can go on writing and survive another five years, living the sort of life he is?"

Francis James looked his professional expressionless self. "Geoffrey's uncle has no serious health affliction. Living alone up there is not normal, but then few men of genius are normal. As long as he has your husband to sustain and encourage him I have every hope he'll go on writing."

She gave Geoffrey a troubled glance. "Which means you could be tied to your uncle in this strange fashion for another five years. It could even become worse and take more of your time."

Geoffrey looked uneasy. "I doubt that. There is always the hope that Uncle Ford will recover mentally to the point where he'll want to live as he did before. Then he wouldn't require my help at all."

"You mustn't count on that," the lawyer rebuked Geoffrey. "It's not fair to build up this young lady's hopes in the light of what we know of your uncle's condition."

Geoffrey met the lawyer's reproachful look with one of his own. "You have neglected another possibility," he said. "My uncle could die."

"That would be the ultimate tragedy," the lawyer said in a bleak tone. "It is our task to see that this does not happen."

"Death is beyond the control of humans," Geoffrey replied.

The lawyer shrugged. "I mean to say we must do all in our power to keep Ford Hunt alive and well."

Enid sighed. "When I came here I had no idea of Ford Hunt's condition or the extent of his dependence on Geoffrey."

Francis James' eyes were cold. "Well, now you know, Mrs. Hunt."

"Yes, now I know," she said quietly.

The lawyer turned to her husband and said, "I'll see you first thing in the morning about those contracts for England, Geoffrey. You can take them up to your uncle when you go over the morning mail with him."

"Very good," Geoffrey said.

Francis James gave them another of his glacial smiles and went on into the house. Once again Enid had the strong impression that the austere lawyer was opposed to her.

She gave her husband a resigned look. "He certainly spelled out the facts for me, didn't he?"

Geoffrey looked embarrassed. "You mustn't mind him. He's very cold. He always has been. But he's made a great success of Uncle Ford's financial affairs."

"I can imagine."

"You'll like him better after you get to know him longer."

"I doubt that," she said dryly. "I don't think he'll let me. He's very aloof."

"He is with everyone."

"Your mother and he seem to get along well."

Geoffrey said, "They're the same age group."

"If he's so valuable to your uncle why is it that he isn't given access to the attic? Why does your uncle restrict himself to seeing only Watts and you?"

"Uncle Ford cares nothing about money," Geoffrey told her. "So none of Francis James' achievements impress him. And I believe they used to argue a lot about details and Uncle Ford found that tiring."

"Suppose you decided you'd had enough and just walked away from all this?" she asked him.

Geoffrey's expression was one of alarm. "I couldn't do that," he protested.

"Why not?"

"I couldn't let Uncle Ford down that way. He needs me."

"So do I."

Her handsome husband looked guilty. "I'll try not to neglect you," he promised. "You knew it would be difficult the first few days we were back."

"I didn't expect anything quite like this," she said. "The whole atmosphere here is so strained. I feel everyone resents me. I talked with Peter again just now and it wasn't a pleasant conversation."

Geoffrey frowned. "What did he say?"

"It's not so much what he says but what he insinuates," she said.

"Tell me."

She shrugged. "He talked about Ellen, your uncle's wife. From the way he spoke he considered you and she were very friendly.

So friendly your uncle objected."

"That's nonsense!"

"Knowing Peter I felt it might be," she said. Though she had a feeling there might be at least a fragment of truth in the rumor. Geoffrey was looking extremely upset at the mention of it.

He said, "Ellen was lonely here. I tried to befriend her. I could see that trouble was developing."

"Was she very attractive?"

"Yes. I'd say so. She had a good mind as well. We often took long walks together. Maybe that's what gave Peter his mistaken idea. We would walk and talk for long periods."

"How did your Uncle Ford feel about this strong friendship between you and his wife?"

"He never mentioned it to me," Geoffrey said. "I'm sure he trusts me even if my brother doesn't."

"He only hinted at all this," she said.

"I don't thank him for it," her husband said curtly. "He was obviously trying to cause trouble between us."

She gave him a searching glance. "It was before you met me. I couldn't be angry if you had an infatuation for this Ellen. It would have been more annoying to Martha."

"They didn't get along," he admitted. "Perhaps there was some jealousy on Martha's part. But she should have understood. In trying to help Ellen I was attempting to stave off the tragedy that followed. If Ellen hadn't killed herself, Uncle Ford wouldn't be in the state he is now either."

Enid smiled wryly, "Then I came along to finish Martha's hopes of marrying you."

"I've told you we had no plans," he protested.

The discussion had ended on the same note as most of their previous ones. She was getting the impression that Geoffrey was doing a kind of verbal shadow-boxing with her. That he was avoiding some of the facts about what had happened in the old house, holding some of its secrets close to him. There was more to his friendship with Ellen than he had revealed, she was sure of that.

They went inside and watched television for a little. Then Geoffrey complained of being weary and they went up to their bedroom. Enid still worried whether or not she should break confidence with Martha and tell him about the almost fatal accident that had taken place on the cliff earlier in the day. But she was almost certain he'd miss the dark implications of what had happened and dismiss it as a harmless incident. So she might as well remain silent.

Geoffrey seemed remote and troubled as they prepared for bed. So much so that she lay awake for a long while worrying about him. She fervently wished that they could both leave the old mansion. But it seemed that Ford Hunt and Cliffcrest had them in their clutches.

Finally she slept. But it was a light sleep marked by blurred, frantic dreams. And then she suddenly awoke with a start. She was filled with a sense of alarm. And turning she was shocked to find the bed empty beside her. Geoffrey had left the bed and wandered off somewhere in the night!

CHAPTER FIVE

Enid listened to hear if he were in the bedroom or the bathroom adjoining it but he wasn't. Perhaps he had wakened and heard some sound in another part of the house and had now gone to find out what it might be. But his absence without any warning worried her. It was almost as if he'd slipped from the bed on some mission he didn't want her to know about.

Or he could have been attracted by some suspicious noise and something have happened to him! Worried, she got out of bed and put on her robe and slippers. Then she went to the door leading to the corridor. She had hesitations about wandering about the gloomy old mansion in the middle of the night. But her concern about Geoffrey overcame them.

Slowly she went out into the blue darkness of the silent hallway. She made her way to the landing and debated which way she would go in further quest of her missing husband. It struck her that he might have been worried about his uncle and so have gone up to the attic retreat where Ford Hunt had locked himself in seclusion.

So she took the stairway leading to the upper region of the old mansion. As she mounted these stairs a gradual, chilling fear took hold of her. Perhaps it was because she felt herself more isolated or because the darkness was more concentrated up there. And there was the overwhelming sense of mystery associated with the recluse poet who had shut himself up there away from everyone else. The thought that he might be afflicted with some sort of madness.

She edged up toward the next landing and was at the top step when she saw the figure watching her from the shadows. She gasped and gripped the railing tighter because it was the phantom, cloaked figure of the ghostly Ellen! The phantom came gliding through the shadows toward her. She could endure it no longer and turned and ran frantically back down the stairs.

She reached her own landing and rather than returning to her bedroom she rushed on down to the ground floor. She was in a panic and desperate to find Geoffrey and tell him what she'd seen on that upper floor. As she stumbled down the remaining stairs she came into collision with a robed Geoffrey on his way up.

He withstood her impact and with an arm around her, asked, "What are you doing up?"

"Looking for you!"

"Why?"

"I missed you! I was afraid something might have happened to you," she managed breathlessly.

He stared at her in the shadows. "That's no reason for you to get upset. To start prowling around the house at night!"

"I couldn't help it. I wouldn't have been able to sleep until I found out where you were."

Geoffrey's arm was still around her and he must have realized she was trembling. "You've surely gotten yourself in a state over it," he said.

"There's more than that," she said. "I went upstairs first, thinking you must have gone up to see your uncle."

"You shouldn't have done that," her husband said sternly.

"I was upset. So I started up and when I reached the landing above ours something horrible happened."

"What?"

"I was met by Ellen's ghost. She blocked my way from going any further!"

"Don't expect me to believe that," he scoffed.

"Just another case of nerves on my part?" she asked bitterly. "Is that what you think?"

"Well?" He sounded exasperated.

"Don't you want to go up there with me? You might see her for yourself."

"I doubt that," he said in a grim voice.

"You won't even go up there?"

"No."

She studied his silhouette in the shadows of the stairs. "I didn't think you'd be so unfair," she told him.

"I'm being sensible."

"You're being smug and narrow-minded."

"Sorry," he said in a stiff voice. "It's time to return to our room. We can't stay here on the stairway arguing until we wake everyone else up."

She allowed him to take her by the arm and guide her up the stairs and then to their room. He had made her feel like a small, foolish child who had needed to be put in her place. It both angered and alarmed her for she knew what she had seen!

In their room Geoffrey shut the door after them and then put on the overhead lights and turned to her. He had a troubled look on his handsome face.

"I hope you don't think I'm being unreasonable," he said.

She regarded him bleakly. "Unless I lie, I'll have to."

"I love you very much," he said. "But I can't allow you to let your juvenile superstition rule you."

Enid shook her head. "There are times when I wonder if you're the same person I met and married in New York. From the moment you arrived here you changed."

He looked uneasy. "More of your too vivid imagination."

"No. It's true!"

He smiled crookedly. "I could say the same thing about you and feel it to be true. These days I don't seem to be able to reach you. You've set yourself against me."

"I hardly ever see you. You spend most of your time in the attic apartment with Ford Hunt. And when you are down here you're different. Now you've started wandering about the house in the night. Why?"

He swallowed hard. "I couldn't sleep."

"Don't tell me your nerves were bothering you?" she said with a hint of sarcasm.

"I wasn't able to sleep. I got up and went downstairs. I thought I'd go to the library and read for a little and when I was weary enough I'd return to bed."

She looked at him accusingly. "There must be something very wrong to upset you this way. To stop you from sleeping!"

He made an impatient gesture with his right hand and turned to move over by the window. "You know it hasn't been easy for me since I got back here."

Enid followed him and stood anxiously at his side. "I'm beginning to be frightened for you," she said. "What does that mad old man demand of you?"

He glanced at her quickly. "Don't call him mad!"

"I think that is what he must be! I can understand grief but not the extremes he's going to. And what kind of homage does he extract for you in return for continuing to turn out his poetry? What kind of slave is this genius uncle of yours trying to make of you?"

Geoffrey had gone pale. He said, "He demands my time and loyalty."

"Your full time and loyalty," she corrected him. "Does he know that you have a wife?"

Geoffrey hesitated. "Why do you ask that?"

"I want to know. Give me a straight answer for a change," she said.

"I haven't told him about my marriage," he said at last.

She stared at his worn face. "Why?"

He took a deep breath. "Various reasons."

"Name a single good one."

"Both Mother and Francis James felt that it might be better not to bother Uncle Ford with the news of my marriage. It takes very little to upset him."

"Why should our marriage upset him?" she demanded.

"Anything that marks any change in the house or in the lives of those close to him bothers him," Geoffrey said earnestly. "You don't understand how close to a mental breakdown he has come and how little it might take to push him over the brink."

Enid listened with a sense of disbelief. It didn't seem possible that Geoffrey had waited this long to tell his famed uncle about them. And it seemed to explain quite a lot to her. She said, "No wonder he has made no allowance for my being here. He doesn't know anything about it."

"We decided it best not to tell him."

"Your mother and that lawyer decided for you," she said. "It's not hard to see that they run things here."

"Not entirely."

"I say different. Your uncle might be less demanding if he knew you had a wife living here."

"It would make no difference with him."

"It's bad enough to live in this ghost-ridden, sinister house without its being kept a secret from its owner," she said.

"I'll tell my uncle when the right moment presents itself," Geoffrey told her in a strained voice.

"And who will decide that? Francis James?"

"Let me take care of it."

She gazed at him in wonder. "How much can you ask of me? How much can you expect from me?"

"I ask your complete faith in me," he said.

"Don't you think you have that?" she asked bitterly. "Why else would I remain here?"

Geoffrey seemed to relent from his stern stand. An expression of tenderness crossed his handsome face and he took her in his arms. "I know I have your love," he said quietly. "I don't deserve it. But if you'll just have a little more patience I'll try to put everything right."

It was a promise which left her exactly nowhere. But the sincerity of his tone and the gentleness of his embrace made her feel she should continue on a little longer. No more was said between them as they returned to bed. It was Geoffrey who fell asleep first.

She heard his regular breathing as she waited for sleep to also come to her. But her troubled thoughts kept it at bay.

She had not been able to investigate the ghost with him. He'd refused to go up and take a look around the upper floor. And as usual he'd rejected the idea of there even being a ghost. It had to be her imagination! And she knew that it wasn't! That she had seen something no matter how much he scoffed.

It had also been shattering to learn that Ford Hunt had not been told of their marriage and didn't even know she was in the house. More and more she was becoming convinced that the famous poet must have become demented after the tragedy of his wife's suicide. Nothing else seemed to explain his absence from the household and the way they catered to him. She was still going over these troublesome matters in her mind when at last sleep gave her a release.

It was suitable to her mood to find the fog had swept in again over night. The thick gray mist which cloaked the old mansion and the surrounding area well matched her own bleak state of mind. Geoffrey said little to her at breakfast and made no reference to the happenings of the previous night. And almost as soon as he'd eaten he went upstairs to be with his uncle.

Left to her own resources Enid began to explore the old mansion. While she knew the attic level was barred to her, she saw no reason why she shouldn't look into the other areas of the big house. She went down the corridor to the rear and found out where the kitchen and the servants' rooms were. The housekeeper, a buxom, pleasant woman seemed to take pleasure in showing her around and pointing out the great fireplace which was now used for charcoal cooking.

On the way back to the front section of the house, she passed the open door of an office-type room and saw that Francis James was seated behind a desk in there intently reading some letter. She passed by without his noticing her. As she reached the other end of the hallway she saw a door which opened on a flight of stairs descending into the cellar.

She went over to the door and saw there was a light on in the cellar. Deciding she would like to see what it was like down there she slowly descended the stairs. The area of the cellar to which they brought her was finished with gray-painted boards and apparently was a storage room. She walked across its rough plank floor to a doorway opening onto a dark, cavernous section.

The moment she stepped through this doorway she felt the entire atmosphere change. It was dank and forbidding in the shadows and everything took on a spectral aspect. She could make out the blurred outlines of ancient furniture and storage crates. No doubt the accumulation of years of living in the old house was set down there. As she moved along in the near darkness she saw still another doorway a distance ahead of her. It was marked by a blur of light.

She felt that familiar uneasiness as she moved towards the doorway. All the phantoms of the old mansion seemed to be gathering to torment her. The remembrance of the cloaked figure of Ellen on the night before vivid in her mind. But she forced herself to go on and finally reached the open doorway.

There was a padlock hung open on its door and seemingly had been unlocked and left there for quickly locking it again. There were winding stone steps leading up from the door. A faint light was coming from some small window far above.

Enid was fascinated by the strangeness of this secret winding staircase and began to climb the stone steps. They were old and worn and she wondered if they had been used regularly in earlier days. Perhaps as far as the ground level of the house. They smelled of dust now and cobwebs clung to the walls so that she just missed brushing her face against them several times.

The circular stairway was weirdly silent and she began to wonder where it would take her. She passed what she was certain must be the ground level but there was no exit. A tiny window a distance above gave off the feeble light in the circular brick-lined tower. The bricks had been painted a light green shade which made it seem a little brighter.

She kept going up the stone steps and each time they wound around she expected to find a door but there was none. Then suddenly she was confronted by a scowling Gertrude Hunt a few steps above her on the way down.

Geoffrey's mother demanded, "How did you get here?"

She was surprised at the anger in the older woman's voice. She said, "I've been wandering around the house and came upon this stairway."

"What were you doing in the cellar?" Geoffrey's mother wanted to know.

"Just looking around."

"Spying would be a better word, wouldn't it?"

Enid felt her cheeks burn as she looked up at the glaring older woman. "I don't know why you say that," she protested. "I just happened to come down to the cellar and see the open door to these stairs."

"There is no need for you to visit the cellar."

"Perhaps not. But I didn't think there was any harm in it."

Geoffrey's mother looked down at her sternly. "This stairway is restricted. It's not open to you. Only myself and Watts ever use it. I must ask you to go back down."

"Very well," Enid said quietly and turned to descend the stairs. She couldn't imagine why Geoffrey's mother was making such a fuss about her being on them but then she knew her to be generally unreasonable.

The older woman accompanied her down as if to make sure she didn't disobey her. She said, "These stairs are rarely used. They are kept locked most of the time."

"Where do they go?" Enid asked.

Geoffrey's mother said, "To the roof. A sort of inside fire escape used in the old days. Further up they have crumbled and are in bad repair. They are unsafe and that is why I wouldn't want you to venture any further on them."

"I see," she said quietly, noting the lame explanation which had been offered. She felt there was no truth in the words of Geoffrey's mother. She was sure the stairway was a secret passage to the attic and that was why the older woman was so opposed to her using it. It might have taken her to the locked quarters of the weird old Ford Hunt. She might even have come face to face with the mysterious poet.

Gertrude Hunt marched sternly down the stairs in her usual determined manner. And when they reached the cellar level she locked the door of the stairway securely. This accomplished, she and Enid went along the length of the cellar.

"You must not come down here again," Geoffrey's mother cautioned her. "It could be very dangerous for you. There are places where you could take a bad fall in the darkness."

"I'll remember that," she said.

"This is a very old house," the older woman went on. "It is impossible to keep it all in perfect repair."

"I suppose Ford Hunt hasn't been able to take much interest in it lately," she volunteered. "With his being ill and confining himself to the attic."

"He is not ill," Gertrude Hunt said curtly.

"And he remains in the attic only because in his old age he has come to set a great value on his privacy."

"I see," she said. Again she had the feeling the older woman was not being truthful.

They reached the stairway to the hall and went up it. Enid felt she had been almost forcibly prevented from making her exploration of the old house. Gertrude Hunt was seemingly determined to remain the dominant figure there.

They moved on along the hallway to the front area of the old mansion. Standing under the crystal chandelier in the big foyer Enid told her mother-in-law, "I understand that Ford Hunt has not been informed of Geoffrey's marriage."

The older woman eyed her belligerently. "What of it?"

"I think he should be."

"Why?"

"For one reason I feel like an interloper in this house with him not knowing about me."

"You shouldn't. Without Geoffrey to assist him the old man couldn't go on writing his poetry. Geoffrey has saved his career."

"I still think Geoffrey's uncle should be told."

"Then we disagree," Gertrude Hunt said coldly. "Francis James is also of the opinion that word of Geoffrey's marriage would only upset his uncle and make him worry that Geoffrey might desert him."

"That won't happen if the situation here is handled properly," she said. "But if it isn't I might feel forced to ask Geoffrey to take me away from here."

Her mother-in-law showed surprise. "Aren't you happy here?"

"Would you call this a happy house?" she asked with some irony in her voice.

"No place is perfect."

"Cliffcrest is far from it," she said. "Geoffrey didn't really explain all I might have to contend with here or my decision about coming would have been different."

The older woman's face was grim. "You can always leave alone. Perhaps you should."

"If I go it won't be alone."

"And I say Geoffrey will not desert his uncle for you," her mother-in-law warned her.

"I believe that is something for Geoffrey himself to decide," she said.

Gertrude Hunt said nothing but glared at her again and then turned and walked back down the hallway in the direction from which they'd just come. Enid stood watching after her and all at once realized she was trembling. Feeling ill and exhausted from the grim exchange with her mother-in-law she walked slowly on to the living room.

There by one of the tall front windows stood Martha staring out at the fog. As Enid approached, Martha turned to her with a knowing smile on her lovely face.

"I heard you having some words with Gertrude," she said slyly.

Enid sighed as she stood beside the dark girl. "More than words, we had a quarrel!"

"You shouldn't mind that. It's fairly common in this house. Gertrude enjoys a lively argument."

"I can't say that I do."

Martha eyed her with cool amusement. "You're much too serious. You aren't equipped to survive in this house. Too many temperaments."

"You're probably right," Enid agreed dolefully.

"Geoffrey will never be free as long as his mother lives," was Martha's warning.

"Has she always dominated him?"

"Yes. Of course since Ford Hunt's upset it has been a lot worse. When the old man was himself he kept her in her place. No one can do that now."

Enid said, "It seems she and that lawyer work hand in glove."

"They understand each other," Martha agreed. "Francis James is clever. Don't underestimate him."

"I don't," she said. "But I'm not going to allow them all to band against Geoffrey and ruin his life and our marriage."

"Do you think you can stop them?"

"I can try," she said firmly. "Wouldn't you have done the same if you'd married Geoffrey?"

Martha gave her another of those mocking smiles. "If I had married Geoffrey everything would have been a lot different."

"In what way?"

"Many ways," the other girl said. "I don't want to go into that. We didn't marry. So it's your problem, isn't it?"

"Yes," she said. "And I'll have to handle it as seems best to me."

"Don't be too ambitious where Gertrude is concerned," was Martha's warning. "She likes to win her battles."

"So do I," Enid said. "And I've had about enough of this frightening old house."

"It's almost like a second home to me."

"I find that hard to understand," she said. "With all the tragedy it has seen and the sense of mystery hanging over it now. I don't know what is wrong with Ford Hunt but it must be tragic to turn a fine intellect such as his into something close to a frightened animal."

"Have you talked to Geoffrey about this?"

"Yes. He won't tell me anything."

Martha nodded. "He has a strong sense of loyalty to his uncle."

"But not the same loyalty to me," Enid said bitterly.

"Geoffrey is under many pressures," the other girl said. "Francis James depends on him to see that Ford Hunt continues to write. That can't be an easy task."

Enid said, "In addition to everything else I saw Ellen's ghost again last night."

Martha at once seemed interested. "Did you?"

"Yes."

"Where?"

"Upstairs. I went to find Geoffrey. He left the room and I didn't know where he'd gone or what was wrong and as I made my way up the stairs in search of him I saw her standing in the shadows on the landing."

"What did you do?"

"I was frozen with fear for a moment. I couldn't do anything."

"And the ghost?"

"She took a step towards me. That broke

the spell. I turned and fled downstairs to find Geoffrey."

"And after that?"

"I found him. I tried to get him to go up and see if the ghost would show herself. He wouldn't."

Martha raised her eyebrows. "Did you expect him to?"

"No. I know he doesn't believe in ghosts."

"So he claims," the pretty dark girl said slyly.

Enid stared at her. "You mean he does?"

"I'd wonder about that particular ghost."

Again Enid felt she was close to getting some new information on the mystery surrounding Ford Hunt, her husband and the old house. She asked, "What do you mean?"

"I don't think Geoffrey would want to meet Ellen's ghost."

"Why especially Ellen's ghost?"

Martha gave her a knowing look. "You know that Ellen was in love with him, don't you?"

"I've heard talk."

"It was true."

"I know," the dark girl said. "I was in love with him as well. She was my only rival at that time."

"What about Geoffrey?"

The dark girl shrugged. "Who can ever be

sure about Geoffrey? He told me he felt sorry for Ellen, a young woman married to an old man in failing health. Maybe that's all it was with him, sympathy."

Enid said, "You sound as if you doubt it?"

"I told you. You can't be sure where Geoffrey is concerned."

"Did Ellen ever talk to you about their friendship?"

"Yes," Martha said. "She was fairly frank in admitting that she loved him."

Enid said, "I still can't think why the fact they were friends, even close friends, would make him want to avoid seeing her ghost."

"You must have heard the rest of the rumor," Martha said mockingly. "That Ellen threw herself from the balcony because of Geoffrey."

It came as a shock. In a small voice, she said, "No. I don't think I've ever heard it said so plainly."

"Most of the people in the house believe that. Perhaps the only one who doesn't is poor old Ford Hunt himself. He apparently has the idea his wife was a suicide because of a quarrel with him."

"And Geoffrey knows this?"

"Of course. Ellen wanted him to run off with her and he refused. He always had more feeling for his famous uncle than anyone else. You might say he knew what was best for him. When Ford Hunt dies Geoffrey will be a rich man. All the family will benefit."

"I see," she said.

"If Geoffrey had run off with Ellen not only Geoffrey but all the others would have lost out. Ford Hunt would have cut them out of his will. You may be sure of that."

"I hadn't realized Geoffrey was directly responsible for her suicide," she said, shocked by the realization.

"Geoff will deny it if you ask him," Martha said in her cynical way. "But that's how everyone else felt about it. So I'd say it has to be true."

CHAPTER SIX

The discussion had become painful for Enid. She told the dark girl, "I somehow wish I hadn't heard about it. And I doubt if it is really true."

Martha looked coldly amused. "Your trust in Geoffrey is touching. I hope he deserves it."

"I think he does," Enid told her and she left the girl standing alone in the living room to go upstairs.

In her own room she paced up and down for a little thinking about the ugly allegations made by Martha against her husband. She knew there was a possibility Martha had told the truth though she hoped this wasn't so. Yet despite her bold front with Martha, she had severe doubts about Geoffrey. He was almost fanatical in his allegiance to his famous uncle. And she had no question that the Hunt family would do all they could to protect the possible inheritance from Ford Hunt.

Had there been an affair between Ellen and Geoffrey? It seemed a likely possibility.

And would Geoffrey coldly turn on Ford Hunt's young wife if he thought his own position in danger of being undermined? This also seemed to be probable. So it could be that because of the various pressures on him Geoffrey had betrayed Ellen and made her take her life. It was an ugly thought but one she could not dismiss. However, until she was sure she wanted to give Geoffrey the benefit of the doubt, Martha could be merely trying to cause trouble between them with her stories.

She moved to the window and saw that her view of the distant ocean was cut off by the fog. She had a limited view of the trees and the lawns below but everything was tinged with the gray mist. She wished that Geoffrey was available to speak to but he was up in the attic with his uncle and she dare not attempt to interrupt him. So she must battle out her grim thoughts alone.

At last she grew so restless she felt she could remain in the room no longer so she put on her light raincoat and a kerchief and started out. She went downstairs and then on to the front verandah. After she stood there a few minutes she decided to cross the fog-shrouded lawns and make her way to the beach. She had an intense desire to be alone and felt this was a place where she might find a welcome solitude.

The grass was wet and though she followed a path across the lawn her shoes gradually became damp. There was a place along the cliffs where weathered wooden steps gave access to the beach. She took the steps down and when she reached the rock-studded sand found the fog just as thick as on the lawns above. She began to stroll along the beach listening to the wash of the waves, a lonely figure.

It was not until a few minutes after she'd begun her aimless walk that she began to feel uneasy. Suddenly she had the feeling she was being watched. That unseen eyes were following her as she made her way down the beach. She turned with frightened eyes and gazed about her. Scanning the rocks for a sign of someone crouching behind them she remained very still. But it was difficult to tell because of the heavy mist.

She began to worry that she had come to the beach on her own. She recalled the accounts she'd heard of the vagrant who'd been seen on the estate. The half-mad tramp who had several times terrified the servants. In her troubled state of mind she'd temporarily forgotten about this threat. Now she remembered and felt anxious.

After a little she decided her nerves had betrayed her. That there was no one following her. Not quite satisfied, she resumed her walk. But now she was a trifle jittery, on edge for any turn of events. She reached a place where she had to climb up over some huge boulders to continue on her way. She clambered up the rocks and was on a high point of them when from directly above her there came a shower of gravel and earth. Startled she at once glanced up and for just a brief flash saw a strange, beard-stubbled face showing over the side of a ledge above her. The eyes in the mottled face had a mad, glaring look which sent terror racing through her. In an instant the face vanished and she was left to wonder whether it had been an illusion or not.

She was sure it hadn't been an illusion and all she could think of was retracing her steps as quickly as she could. She got down from the rocks and started hurrying across the expanse of beach in the direction of the steps which would take her back to the lawns of Cliffcrest. But now the distance seemed endless. The wash of the waves took on a sinister sound and the fog-laden beach had become a place of phantoms.

Then, emerging from the fog, she saw a strange figure coming toward her. She halted and gasped not knowing whether to turn and run in the opposite direction or to move down nearer the water and try and avoid a confrontation with the newcomer in this manner. Then neither method seemed feasible. So she stood there miserably speculating whether this would turn out to be the terrifying character that had stared down at her from the rocks.

As the man came closer she saw that it wasn't the same one who'd been spying on her earlier. This was a young man in a tweed suit with a rather pleasant if hollow-cheeked face.

Coming up within a couple of feet of her he said, "I couldn't imagine anyone else would be walking down here."

She swallowed hard. Relieved by his harmless appearance and manner. "Nor could I. I had a fright earlier. An ugly face stared down at me from the cliffs."

"Is that so?" he sounded interested. "Did you recognize the fellow?"

"No. But from the descriptions I've heard I'd say he was a tramp who's been loitering around the grounds. Others have seen him."

"You can't be too careful," was his advice.

"I know," she agreed.

"You get a lot of strange people along this

coast these days. They drift up or down from the cities and camp along the way," the young man said.

"So it seems," she said.

"By the way I'm not a travelling hippie," the young man informed her in a genial tone. "My name is Drake Winslow and I own a cottage next to the Hunt estate. I assume you're a Hunt?"

She managed a smile. "I'm married to one."

"Which one?"

"Geoffrey."

The young man lifted his eyebrows. "I didn't know he was married."

"It happened lately." She could feel him staring at her, appraising her.

Drake Winslow said, "I offer you my congratulations. I've only met a brother of your husband's. His name is Peter if I'm not mistaken."

"Yes," she said, wondering what his impression had been of Peter.

"And there's a girl lives there. Her name is Martha something and she paints."

"That's right," she agreed. "So you're not a stranger to us."

"The meetings have been very casual. I'm not sure they'll recall me," the brown-haired man said.

Because Enid regarded him as an ideal type, she couldn't imagine the others not remembering him. She asked, "What are you doing here?"

He showed a smile on his pleasant face. "I'm an artist. I was working with one of the Hollywood studios. I've had enough of that. I made up my mind to come here and do some honest painting."

"It sounds like a wonderful resolve. Have you done much?"

Drake Winslow shook his head. "I'm too taken up by the beauty of my surroundings. It has stunned me artistically for a little. Later on I may snap out of it and be able to continue working. Just now I stroll around and marvel."

"You can't see much on a day like this."

"No," he said. "But I find even this thick fog fabulous. I hear we get more of it than any other spot along the coast with the sole exception of San Francisco."

"I'm not an authority," she said. "But I have been warned about the fog."

He looked at her with a quizzical smile. "Still you must like it or you wouldn't be down here."

"It has a kind of morbid fascination for me," she admitted.

"What about Cliffcrest?" he asked.

She hesitated. "It's very large and quite ugly."

"I agree. I hear it is phantom-ridden as well. Do you know anything about it?"

Enid studied him for a long moment before she replied, "There is talk about the house. And because of its sad history I think it may be haunted."

"You sound as if you'd seen some of the ghosts?"

"I can't reply truthfully. I think I may have."

"Well, that's something," he said.

"Don't quote me, please!" she begged him.

"You wish to take it back?"

"No," she said. "It's just that they're rather touchy about it at Cliffcrest."

Drake was staring hard at her. As if he might be trying to decide something about her. "Very well," he said. "We'll keep the ghosts a dark secret."

"It would be better."

He said, "There is something truly scary about that old mansion. And I hear no one ever sees Ford Hunt anymore. How do you account for that?"

She felt there was more to his question than there seemed on the surface. She said, "He hasn't been well. Not since his wife's suicide. I understand it shocked him ter-

126

ribly. He's been a recluse since then."

"But that was some time ago," the young man persisted. "You'd think he'd have recovered by now."

"He still stays in his attic apartment. My husband and a servant are the only ones he will see."

Drake was listening avidly. "Surely he expressed a desire to meet you?"

"No." She didn't think she should reveal that the poet didn't know of her marriage to his nephew.

"That's odd. Geoffrey marrying could be considered a major event. And you claim his uncle has shown no interest?"

"Not as yet. He may later when he's better."

"Yes, there's his illness to be considered," Drake Winslow agreed. "But his bad health doesn't seem to have hurt his poetry. In the last couple of years, at a time when he'd almost been forgotten by the public and critics, he began writing poetry for our age. He's done some of his best work lately."

She managed a forlorn smile. "It could be the solitude has helped his work."

"Possibly," the expatriate Hollywood artist said. "Anyhow I'll venture that he's made more money in the past few years than he ever did before."

"I think that's true. My husband said something about it."

"I must meet your husband," Drake Winslow said.

"Yes."

"I believe the brother I know is rather a different type."

"Peter is. He's had some personal problems but he's much better these days."

Drake gave her a wise look. "I know. I'm familiar with his history of heroin addiction. Too bad. He has a brilliant mind and he plays an excellent piano."

"So I've been told."

"He gave me the impression that Geoffrey was interested in this Martha who lives at Cliffcrest much of the time. That's why I was surprised to hear you'd married him."

"A lot of people did expect he'd marry Martha," she agreed.

He stood there a rather romantic figure in the thick fog, his curly brown hair wet with mist. And he said, "Wasn't there also someone else?"

She said, "I can't be sure."

"You must know about Ellen," he insisted.

She played innocent. "You mean his uncle's late wife?"

He nodded. "The girl who threw herself

to her death from the balcony up there."

"Yes. What about her?"

"Peter claims his brother and Ford Hunt's wife were in love."

"Peter is a twisted, bitter person who says a lot of rash things."

"So you're denying the story?"

"I can't tell you anything," she said. "That was some years ago. I wasn't here."

His brown eyes widened with surprise. "And your husband has never discussed that phase of his life with you?"

"No."

"I'm surprised."

"Why should he? He may be sensitive about it," she said. "He probably just doesn't want to be reminded of those days. Martha would know more about it than I do." She had decided if he wanted information he'd have to get it elsewhere. She was not going to repeat the several accusations which Martha had made to the effect that Geoffrey had been responsible for Ellen's suicide.

Drake seemed almost to read her thoughts. He said quietly, "I understand. I'm sorry I brought it up. It was the talk about ghosts did it. According to Peter the ghost of Ellen has been seen at Cliffcrest."

"It's become a sort of legend," she agreed without definitely committing herself.

"Yes," he glanced up at the mist-covered cliffs. "You think you saw the stranger up there?"

"I saw someone."

"Not a pleasant-looking type?"

"Not at all."

"You shouldn't be left alone," Drake Winslow said. "No telling what sort he is."

"His eyes had a mad light in them."

"Sounds typical. I'll see you back to Cliffcrest."

She was grateful for the suggestion but didn't want to bother him. She said, "I don't want to be a nuisance."

"You're not being a nuisance," he said. "I'd feel guilty if I didn't see you home."

They started back along the beach together in the thick fog. He talked about his painting and what he planned to do in the months ahead. She found him a completely interesting person. They climbed the wooden steps to the top of the cliffs and then he strolled with her until the outline of Cliffcrest showed through the mist.

He halted and smiled. "I guess this will see you safely in."

"Yes," she said. "I'll manage nicely from here."

"I've enjoyed meeting you," the young artist told her.

"And I can't say how fortunate I was that you came along when you did. I was very frightened down there alone."

He looked serious. "I wouldn't be in a hurry to do that again."

"I won't. I thought in daylight I'd be safe."

"The beach is lonely at this point," Drake Winslow said. "And the fog is so heavy it might as well be night."

"That's so," she agreed. "I'd like to have you come in and meet my husband sometime."

"Thank you."

"I'd invite you in now," she apologized, "but it's likely he'd still be up with his uncle. He spends a lot of the time up there. The old man won't work unless Geoffrey is around to encourage him."

"Interesting."

"And rather unfortunate," she sighed. "It means I see very little of my husband."

"That could be awkward," the artist agreed. "Well, let us hope we'll meet soon again."

"We must," she said, extending her hand to him. "And once more, thank you."

They parted with Drake Winslow going back to the steps leading to the beach while she went towards Cliffcrest. Her mind was filled with thoughts of what had gone on down there and the young man who had come to her aid. She felt almost sure she might have been attacked by that mad-looking stranger who'd been following her if Drake hadn't turned up.

She went up the several steps to the verandah and entered the foyer of the old mansion. As she closed the door behind her she saw Geoffrey coming down the broad stairway with a grim expression on his handsome face.

"Geoffrey!" she exclaimed. "If I'd known you were coming down I'd have invited in a young man I met on the beach."

Her husband had reached the bottom of the stairs. "Who was he?" he demanded abruptly.

"A young artist. His name is Drake Winslow. He lives near here."

"Why did you make friends with him?" Geoffrey asked coldly.

She was astonished by his attitude. "I was on the beach alone and someone began following me."

"That fellow?"

"No! The one the servants have been complaining about. The mad-looking man who's been lurking around the estate."

"Go on," her husband said in the same icy fashion.

"I knew I was being followed. Then when I stopped once this man betrayed himself by knocking some earth and gravel down from the spot on the cliffs from which he was spying on me. I looked up and got a glimpse of him. He was horrible looking."

"You'd never seen him before?"

"Never. I was terrified. And I knew I had a long way to get back here. It was then that Drake came along."

"You say he lives near here?"

"Yes. That's how he happened to be on the beach. He also says he's met both Martha and Peter."

Geoffrey frowned. "If he's a friend of Peter's, that robs him of his reputation at once."

"I'd hardly call that fair," she protested.

"It's been true from past experience," her husband said.

"He also knows Martha."

"I'll ask her about him," her husband said.

"Why make such a fuss about it?" she demanded. "I was lucky to have him come along."

Her husband's face had a stubborn look. "Perhaps."

"You know I was," she insisted.

"Perhaps he intended the meeting to take

place," was Geoffrey's insinuation.

"That's nonsense," she rebuked him.

He continued to study her fixedly. "You two seemed to be having a good time together for strangers."

"We were friendly. Is that wrong?"

"It depends."

She stared at him in shock. "I'm sorry now you weren't upstairs and then I'd have missed this third degree."

"It's not a third degree."

"It seems like one to me," she told him. And she tried to get by him but he blocked her way.

"You're surely determined to behave childishly," she complained.

"I suppose he was the perfect gentleman."

"As a matter of fact, yes," she said.

Geoffrey's eyes were blazing. "I don't want you seeing him again."

She gave her husband a defiant look. "I won't make any such promise."

"And I'll not have you fraternizing with trespassers," he told her.

"He wasn't a trespasser!"

"He was on our beach!" Geoffrey informed her angrily.

She shook her head. "I hate you when you behave this way," she said unhappily and she brushed by him and hurried up the stairs to her room.

There were tears in her eyes when she threw herself on the bed. It had been a stupid, needless scene caused by Geoffrey's arrogance. An arrogance which resembled his mother's to a frightening degree. She had been upset enough before but the exchange had left her in a true depression. She couldn't understand Geoffrey's jealousy being so easily aroused.

And then she began to worry whether it was jealousy which had made him so wary or something else. Fear, perhaps! Was Geoffrey afraid of strangers because he feared they might find something about him and the doings at the old mansion which would spell trouble for him? Had he truly something to conceal about Ellen Hunt's suicide?

It had made no difference to him that the young man had known both Peter and Martha. Geoffrey had chosen to go on in this truly ridiculous fashion. She began to wonder if she had made a bad mistake in her marriage and in coming to Cliffcrest. It was the old mansion which had seemed to cast a shadow over their marriage. Everything had changed since their arrival at the sinister house. Geoffrey had come to seem like a different person under his uncle's influence.

The more she thought about it the more she felt she must somehow get to talk to Ford Hunt and tell the old poet the true state of affairs in the old mansion. She lay stretched out on the bed for some time. Then she heard the door open gently and she looked up to see it was her husband who had come into the room.

He stood very still and pale-faced in the middle of the room. Then in an almost expressionless voice, he told her, "I've come to tell you I'm sorry and to ask your forgiveness."

She sat up and stared at him. "You might have thought of that before you caused the scene."

"I was stupid," he said, his tone weary. "I know that now."

"Why did you behave that way?"

"I didn't like seeing you in his company," Geoffrey said.

She got to her feet facing him. She was now becoming suspicious of his sudden about-face. And of his abject apology in this agonized manner.

She said, "I think there was more to it than that."

"What could there be?" He sounded frightened.

"You want to keep everyone away from here, deny me having any friends," she said. "Why?"

"You're imagining those things."

"No," she said firmly. "It's as if you had something you wanted to hide. Something you're terrified people will find out. Has it to do with what happened to your uncle's wife? Is it something to do with her suicide?"

"You're confusing issues," her husband protested. "You always do. I come to you with a sincere apology and you won't accept it."

"I'll accept it if it is sincere," she said quietly. "And I've made up my mind to something else. If we're to save our marriage we have to be honest with each other."

"Haven't we been?"

"I'm not sure you have," she said. "In fact I know you haven't. Your Uncle Ford hasn't been told about our marriage. I want that to be corrected. I demand that you take me up to meet him and that you tell him about us."

Geoffrey looked aghast. "Impossible!"

"No," she said.

"You have no idea what you're asking," Geoffrey protested. "I have explained the state he's in. Giving him that kind of shock could ruin everything."

"You refuse, then?"

"I have no choice," he said.

"You expect me to remain here?"

"I want you to."

"Then you'd better think over what I've said," she told him quietly. "I want to see your uncle and let him understand that your loyalty is due me first."

Geoffrey came to her and caught her by the arms. "Don't try to force me to do things that are beyond my ability!"

"Why didn't you marry Martha?" she asked with tear-filled eyes. "Why didn't you bring her the unhappiness you've brought me?"

"I love you," he told her. "I love you in a way I never loved Martha. You must believe that."

She looked at him with fear in her eyes. "Then tell me what is wrong here? What evil is going on in this house? What awful secret are you all hiding?"

He stared at her in anguished silence. "Listen to me," he pleaded. "Have faith in me!"

"I feel as if I've made a pact with the Devil," she told him in a choked voice. "As if I've become part of your wickedness by just standing by silently."

"There's no need of you feeling that

way," he told her. "Just have faith in me a little longer." And he took her in his arms and holding her tight to him kissed her.

It ended as usual with nothing changed and nothing settled. Enid went down to join the others at dinner with a feeling of utter despair. All during the meal she felt uneasy. She had an idea they all knew about the quarrel she'd had with Geoffrey and were relishing it. Again the strong impression that they were all against her grew on her.

When she left the table Peter Hunt came sidling up to her with one of his sneering smiles. The long-haired brother of her husband said, "You're looking very tense tonight."

She eyed him angrily. "What do you care?"

"You married the wrong brother," he said mockingly. "I keep telling you, but you won't believe it. You'll never have any happiness with Geoffrey."

"What do you know about it?"

The long-haired young man eyed her with insolence. "I know my brother and his obligations."

She frowned. "Tell me, what are his obligations? Why can't he be free of his Uncle Ford? Why should he continue on here at his beck and call?"

Peter laughed. "You'll find out one day."

"You could tell me now."

"It wouldn't do any good if I did," was his answer. "Your best bet is to leave brother Geoffrey — whether you believe it or not."

It was close to what she was thinking herself. But she did not want to give him the satisfaction of knowing it. So she said, "I'll make up my own mind about that."

"If I were you I wouldn't take too long about it," Peter taunted her.

She said, "At least there is one thing you can tell me. I met a young man today, a Drake Winslow. He knows both you and Martha. What can you tell me about him?"

Peter's eyebrows raised. "Drake Winslow?"

"Yes," she said. "He lives in a cottage down the shore."

A strange look had come across the face of the long-haired Peter. He said, "He used to live down the shore."

"Where does he live now?"

"He doesn't live anywhere," Peter said in his sneering fashion. "He was murdered seven years ago."

CHAPTER SEVEN

Enid had not been prepared for this reply. She stared at Peter thinking it might be another of his macabre jokes but she saw at once that it was not. He meant what he said. Drake Winslow was dead! But she had walked on the beach and talked with Drake Winslow only a few hours ago.

"There must be some mistake," she gasped.

"I only know of one Drake Winslow who lived along this coast and he was murdered. He used to visit here."

"Visit here?"

"Yes. He was a friend of Ellen's. They knew each other before she married Uncle Ford," Peter said.

"Then he would know this place and Geoffrey would know him!" she exclaimed.

"Of course Geoffrey would know him." He gave her one of his mocking smiles. "So you met a dead man on the beach today, did you?"

"I don't know," she said, touching a hand to her temple. "I'm completely confused."

"You must be if you met Drake Winslow."

She eyed Peter sharply. "You say this Drake Winslow was murdered. What happened?"

"Someone broke into his cottage one night and clobbered him over the head with a golf club. A day woman came and found him unconscious on the floor the next morning. She phoned the police and an ambulance. But by the time they got him to the hospital he was dead."

"And they never found the killer?"

"He wasn't able to tell them anything about it," Peter said. "And whoever did it left no clues. They wore gloves and were careful in every other way."

"So it was an unsolved murder," she said in a small voice.

The long-haired Peter nodded. "That's right. Ellen was very broken up about it. She was fond of Drake. I liked him too. He was a good sport. I was on the stuff then and whenever I needed some extra money he gave it to me."

She gave him a searching look. "Are you taking drugs now, Peter?"

His smile was mocking. "Clean as an early morning snow." He glanced at his watch. "I must be on my way. I like to be at the lounge early."

"I want to hear more about Drake Winslow," she said.

He gave her one of his wise looks. "Ask Martha or Geoffrey, they can tell you." And he left her.

She went into the living room in search of Geoffrey and found his mother seated there in conversation with Francis James. They both stopped talking and gazed at her as she entered the room.

Feeling she was intruding on them, she said apologetically, "I'm looking for my husband."

Francis James was on his feet now. "He had to go up and be with Ford Hunt for a while. The old man is trying to finish a poem for a publishing deadline tomorrow."

She said, "Then there's no telling how long he'll be up there?"

"No," the gray-faced lawyer said.

"My advice to you is go to bed when you feel like it," Gertrude Hunt spoke up. "There's every likelihood Geoffrey will be up there late."

"I suppose so," she said with a sigh. "Thank you." And she left the room. They did not resume their talk while she was within hearing distance.

She left them with the feeling that what they'd been discussing had something to do with the sinister happenings at Cliffcrest. She was growing more bewildered and upset as time went by. This latest news that she had been talking to a dead man meant only one thing, she'd been taken in by an impostor. But why should anyone turn up on the beach and deliberately pose as a man murdered years before. He must realize he'd be found out.

Perhaps that was it. That he wanted to be found out. Now she began to realize why Geoffrey had been so upset. While he hadn't admitted it to her, he'd known that she'd been talking to an impostor. She'd told him the man's name as soon as she went in the house. It had been after that Geoffrey had reacted so badly.

She started up the stairs on her way to their room. When she reached the first landing she met Martha. The dark haired girl gave her a wise smile.

"If you're looking for Geoffrey you'd better give up. He's in the attic with Ford Hunt."

"I know."

Martha asked her, "Were you ever out on the balcony from which Ellen is supposed to have leapt to her death?"

"No."

"Let me show you," Martha said at once.

"Come along." And she led the way up another stairway and then along a broad corridor to French doors. She opened one of the doors and stepped outside onto the balcony. Enid joined her and saw that the balcony was about six feet long and three feet deep. They were high above the ground and the distant ocean reflecting the starlit sky seemed not too far distant.

"This is the balcony," Martha said, staring out towards the ocean.

Enid gave a tiny shiver. "It's not a large balcony. And it's cold out here tonight."

"The fog vanishes when it gets this cold," Martha said. "This is a typical California night."

"Even with the fog this afternoon it wasn't this chilly," she remembered.

"I know," Martha agreed. She glanced down. "It's a long way to the ground."

Enid forced herself to look down. "Yes."

"There was a scream. And the next thing her body was hurtling down. She just slipped over the railing. You can see that it wouldn't be difficult."

And by way of illustrating this Martha all at once grasped Enid by the shoulders and forced her over the balcony. She screamed. For seconds it seemed as if she'd gone too far and would surely topple over. Then

Martha pulled her back and released her.

Enid turned on the dark girl angrily. "What made you do a mad thing like that?"

Martha opened her palms in lieu of an explanation. "I don't know. I was carried away. I wanted you to see how easy it was for Ellen to end it all."

"I almost lost my balance and fell down there myself!"

"You were in no danger," Martha said calmly. "I had no intention of letting go of you."

"You might have accidentally," Enid reproved her. "It wasn't a good joke!"

"It wasn't meant to be," the other girl said soberly. "I merely wanted to point out that the balcony made an excellent suicide spot. I'd use it myself if I ever came to that state of mind."

Enid shivered again and this time it was more because of the other girl's words and not because of the night. She said, "Let's go in."

In the shadowed hallway she turned to Martha and asked her, "What can you tell me about Drake Winslow?"

The other girl started a little, enough so that it could be noted that she reacted with shock even in the near-darkness. In a cautious tone she said, "What do you want to know about him? How he died?"

"For one thing, yes."

"He was murdered," Martha said with a full return to her old haughty manner. "You must have heard about it."

"Not before. He used to visit here?"

"He came to see Ellen. Her husband disliked him. Somehow Drake always seemed to run into him. The funny part being it was so annoying for them both."

"Had Drake been here the night of his murder?"

"As a matter of fact, yes," Martha said. "He was here that night. I saw Ellen shepherd him off into one of the downstairs side rooms and close the door behind them. Those two were close. Everyone knew that."

"Ellen appears to have had lots of lovers."

"I'm afraid so. Drake Winslow was the first and then came Geoffrey. The old man had a difficult problem guarding his property. It's small wonder he later had a breakdown."

"Then it was a serious affair between Ellen and this Drake?"

"Yes," the other girl said, the shadows hiding the expression on her face. "And serious enough between her and Geoffrey."

"Let's concentrate on her affair with

Drake," Enid suggested.

"Whatever you say."

"It seems she must have been bold about it."

"Ellen wasn't one to pretend. At least she had that virtue."

"What about Drake Winslow?"

"He was an artist without too much money. And he had plenty of charm. Ellen liked young men with charm."

"Then why did she marry Ford Hunt who was an older man?"

"She saw a chance to benefit herself," Martha said with scorn. "It was a big step up in the world for her. She knew Ford was on the brink of making a lot of money from his poetry. And she wanted to be the wife of a famous poet. Not Ford's wife, you understand, but a famous poet's wife. And so she was able to fulfill this role through marriage with an elderly man she didn't love."

Enid said, "How cruel she must have been!"

"I'd say so," the dark girl agreed. "Ford told her to tell Drake not to come here. But he didn't pay any attention, if, in fact, she ever told him."

"You don't think she did?"

"No."

"What then?" Enid asked.

"The affair went on with everyone knowing. Ford Hunt threatened to divorce Ellen but we all felt he wouldn't. He prized his young wife too much, even being willing to allow an occasional discreet infidelity on her part. But Ellen pushed it too far."

"And?"

"Drake Winslow was murdered," Martha said. "What a waste of youth and charm! He was charming."

"So you said," Enid agreed, anxious to get on to other matters before Martha left her. "Why do you think he was killed? It was seemingly not mere theft that was the motive."

"Someone waited until he went home with too much to drink. He often got that way. And then they took one of his golf clubs and beat him over the head until he died as the result of his injuries."

"And no one knew who did it?"

The girl in the shadowed corridor gave a tiny grim laugh. "At least no one would say who they thought was responsible."

"Why?"

"They had reasons," Martha said. "Perhaps not all the same. But they added up."

Enid said, "It could have been someone in this house."

"Too bad Ellen isn't alive to hear you say

that," Martha taunted her. "She would surely appreciate it."

"Then someone here did kill Drake?"

"Ask Geoffrey," she said. "I'm tired. I'm going to my room." And she started away down the corridor to vanish in the darkness.

Enid stood there by herself feeling lost. Stumbling on this murder story was even more fantastic than her finding out about Ellen's suicide. And she was convinced the two events were linked in some way. What worried her the most was the implication on Martha's part that Geoffrey might be the killer. She'd hinted it very broadly.

Perhaps the basis for the rumor was sound. Geoffrey had been in love with Ellen and he disliked Drake Winslow. If he found out Ellen was on the point of running away with him he might have felt forced to act. And out of this decision might have come the murder.

If Geoffrey had killed the artist this explained many things. And perhaps it was fear of discovery, or remorse for the part she'd played in the killing which had made Ellen take her own life. The wayward girl had not been able to see any other way out. It seemed the answer to the riddle.

Enid glanced toward the open French door onto the balcony and decided to close it. She went over and carefully shut the door trying not to think of that night of desperation when a distraught Ellen had gone over the railing.

She moved down the dark corridor to the landing and the stairway to the floor below where their bedroom was. As she made her way down she heard a footstep on the stair behind her. It made her heart jump. She turned quickly to look up into the gaunt face of the elderly Watts. He had an empty tray in his hands.

"I didn't know who it was," she told the elderly servant.

"My apologies, Mrs. Hunt," Watts said at once.

"Is my husband still busy up there?" she asked.

"Yes, Ma'am," the gaunt-faced hunchback said.

"Ford Hunt is working?"

"Yes. He often prefers the evening and late night for his writing," Watts said as they reached the landing.

She gave him a thoughtful look. "Have you been employed by Ford Hunt long?"

"Quite a few years."

"You must have seen many changes in him," she said.

"I have," he agreed.

"Would you consider him well?"

The gaunt, sallow face of the hunchback showed concern. "No. He is not well. I have watched him fail steadily."

"But he is still able to get around?"

"Oh, yes. He's not all that ill."

"And he'll see no one but my husband and you?"

"That is correct," Watts said with a trace of pride. "He knows he can trust us."

"Isn't his locking himself up in this fashion carrying things too far?"

"My employer is a strange man," Watts told her gravely. "And not to be judged by ordinary standards."

"Of course that is true," she agreed. "Most artistic people are difficult to understand."

"Yes, Mrs. Hunt," Watts agreed and with a nod he moved on.

She went down the dimly lit corridor to their bedroom. There she waited for Geoffrey and debated all that she'd just heard. She kept wondering who the man she'd met on the beach was. She didn't believe in ghosts so it must have been an impostor. Yet suppose she was wrong. What a macabre revelation that would be!

Martha had terrified her physically by projecting her over the balcony railing and tormented her mentally by suggesting that Geoffrey might have been the murderer of Drake Winslow. She had known from the first that the dark girl was not her friend, now it became clearer than ever.

She sat in the easy chair by the window and stared up at the high ceiling with its ornate light fixture. What was she to do? How could she hope to salvage her marriage from this dark mixture of doubts and unsolved mysteries? She could not picture Geoffrey as a killer. Yet in his home surroundings, he had turned out to be a much different person from the man she'd met in New York. So it was all too possible there could be many things about him she did not understand.

The door opened and it was her husband. Geoffrey came into the room looking weary and tense as he had so many times before. He said, "You've waited up for me."

"Yes. Didn't you want me to?"

He came over by her chair. "It wouldn't have mattered. You could have gone to bed."

"I was worried about you," she said. "Slaving up there with that eccentric old man."

"I don't mind it."

"You look exhausted."

Geoffrey sighed. "At least the night's work turned out well. The manuscript will be ready for the publisher tomorrow. I think it may be one of his finest poems."

She studied her handsome husband with concern. "There's something I must ask you about."

"What?"

"Earlier today when I told you the man I met on the beach was Drake Winslow you didn't contradict me."

Geoffrey showed no betraying expression. "So?"

She stood up. "I know now that it wasn't Winslow. It couldn't have been. He was murdered some years ago."

"Who told you?"

"Martha and Peter. Why didn't you say anything?"

He seemed grimly resigned. "You were so sure it was Drake Winslow I didn't want to spoil the illusion."

"You saw the man. Do you know who it was?"

"No. He was a stranger to me."

"Why?"

"Why what?"

Her pretty face showed perplexity. "Why should anyone play such a mad prank on me? Pretend to be a dead man."

"I'm sure I don't know," her husband said coldly.

"He seemed to know a lot about Cliffcrest and all of you," she said.

"So it seems."

She was watching her husband closely. "Do you suppose it was someone investigating Drake Winslow's murder?"

"Perhaps. It's rather late for that. More than seven years."

"But often they leave cases open until some new evidence turns up. Could they have found some new evidence and started another investigation?"

"What new evidence could there be?" he asked, his tone icy.

Flustered, she said, "I can't imagine."

Geoffrey frowned. "Whoever it was knew something of the past here."

"Yes."

"It wouldn't have to be the police. It could be a friend of Drake Winslow's."

"But what a strange thing to do. To pretend to be a dead man."

"He may have had some reason for it."

"What?"

"He knew you'd come back here and tell me. Perhaps he wanted my reaction. Or the reaction of someone else in the house."

"Would you know him if you saw him

again?" she asked.

Her husband shook his head. "No. Frankly I didn't see his face clearly. You were a distance from the house and it was foggy at the time. I couldn't tell what he looked like."

His words sent a chill through her. She gave him a frightened glance. "Then perhaps I was talking to a ghost! A ghost that came out of the fog!"

Geoffrey smiled wryly. "Aren't you the one who doesn't believe in ghosts?"

"This makes me wonder."

"I'd say the chances are we're dealing with a real person."

She said, "You knew him well, didn't you?"

"Yes."

"How did you feel about him?"

"I didn't like him."

Her eyes met his. "Martha claims he and Ellen were very close."

Geoffrey looked bleak. "Is that of any importance now?"

"She seemed to think so."

"I don't," her husband said shortly.

"Martha also hinted that you might have been the one who murdered Drake Winslow out of jealousy."

There was a long moment of silence between them. Then Geoffrey said, "Are you sure?"

"Yes."

"Do you think I might be a murderer?"

She shook her head. "No. But I know so little of what went on here then. So many things have turned up about those days. I feel I'm still in the dark."

"I can't see what you have to gain by delving into the past," he said.

"At least I'd understand what is going on around me now better," she said.

"Why not be content to be on the sidelines? You'd be better off."

"Because I don't want people insinuating you are a murderer," she said. "I want to silence them."

His smile was grim. "That won't be easy."

"When did you last see Drake Winslow?"

His brow furrowed. "The night of his murder. He was here visiting Ellen for a while."

"Did you talk with him?"

Geoffrey hesitated, then he said, "Yes."

"What did you say?"

"I warned him that Ford Hunt was very upset about his relationship with Ellen and wouldn't put up with it much longer. I pointed out that the old man was on the verge of a breakdown."

She asked, "What was his reply?"

Her husband looked uncomfortable. "He was unreasonable."

"In what way?"

"He told me I wasn't speaking for Ford Hunt but for myself. That I was the one concerned about Ellen while pretending it was her husband."

"And?"

"I told him he was wrong. And I advised him to stay away from Cliffcrest."

"Then what?"

"He left without giving me any satisfaction," Geoffrey said. "I never saw him alive again."

"What about Ellen?"

"She was very broken up by his murder. I don't think she ever got over it. It wasn't too long afterward that she took her own life."

"Did the police question you all?"

"They came here and asked some questions at the time. In the end they seemed to decide that it had been a robbery attempt and murder came into it."

Enid asked her husband, "Do you agree?"

"The police should know better than anyone."

"That isn't always so," she pointed out quietly.

"I believe it to be in this case," Geoffrey said.

"What does Ford Hunt think?"

Geoffrey looked uneasy again. "He doesn't ever discuss it with me."

"I find that strange."

He turned away from her. "Why?"

"You are the one member of the family he confides in. Surely he'd have some comment to offer to you on the subject."

"I'd say he wants to put the whole affair out of his mind. Forget about it."

"That can't be easy for him."

"It's not," her husband said. "I think it's time we dropped this discussion and got ready for bed."

"I had to hear your side of it."

"Now you have."

"And I feel as if you'd only told me part of what I should know," she complained.

"I can't help that," he said shortly.

She went to him and touched a hand on his arm. "You know all this matters only because I care for you."

"I wonder," he said staring down at her.

"It's true. If I didn't love you, I'd leave Cliffcrest this minute and begin arrangements for a divorce."

"Perhaps you should do just that."

"And desert you? Never."

"Thank you," it was said in a tone somewhere between gratitude and mockery.

"I mean it," she said sincerely.

He bent and touched his lips to hers lightly. But it was a gesture rather than a kiss of feeling. A duty prompted by her words of devotion. His action left her more unhappy than if he hadn't done it.

They began preparing for bed. She finished first and was back in the bedroom while Geoffrey remained in the bathroom cleaning his teeth. She went to the window and saw that the fog had still not returned. The night was clear and cold as it had been earlier.

Geoffrey came to her. "I hope your mind is at rest," he said.

She glanced up at his bronzed face. "In a sort of way."

He smiled. "Have some faith in me. Nothing here is as bad as it seems."

"It's a house filled with ghosts!" she exclaimed emotionally. "Ugly phantoms of the past reaching out to spoil things for us."

"They won't unless we allow them to," he told her.

She was on the point of telling him how Martha had terrified her on the balcony by pretending to push her over and of the earlier incident with the car when the dark girl had almost run her down. It seemed unwise to hide this from him any longer. But before she could bring this up her eyes caught the movement of a shadowy figure on the lawn.

"Look!" she cried, taking Geoffrey's arm to get his attention. "Down there!"

"What?" he peered out the window with her.

She pointed. "By the bushes. I just saw a man. He darted out of sight. I think it's the same one I met on the beach today. The one who called himself Drake Winslow."

Geoffrey was frowning. "Are you sure?"

"Yes."

"Then I'm going down to have a look," her husband said grimly. "I'd like to have a chat with that gentleman."

She held onto his arm. "Better not. There might be danger!"

"I'll risk that," was Geoffrey's reply as he drew away from her and started for the door.

"Geoffrey, please!" she called after him. But he was already out of the room. She knew she must follow him even though she had only her robe over her nightgown to protect her against the cold night. Without hesitation she ran across the room after him.

CHAPTER EIGHT

Geoffrey had already vanished down the stairway by the time she reached the landing. She followed him breathlessly terrified of what might happen when he pursued the furtive figure of the stranger on the lawn. Geoffrey had left the front door open behind him and she ran straight out onto the verandah. She hesitated for a moment trying to discover where he'd gone.

Then she saw him racing toward the cliffs in the darkness. She went down the verandah steps and started after him. She was a third of the way across the lawn when from the bushes on her left there appeared an apparition. It was the familiar ghostly figure of Ellen! The phantom in the flowing cloak glided menacingly toward her.

Enid halted, her path cut off by the ghost. She dodged to the right and tried to escape the phantom but wasn't successful. The clutching hands of the weird figure caught her and she fell forward onto the grass.

"Help!" she screamed as she tried to escape the phantom.

"Enid!" It was Geoffrey calling back. He seemed not too far away.

"Here!" she cried again.

At the same instant the phantom took cover in the bushes once more. By the time Geoffrey came running back Enid was lifting herself from the moist grass.

"What happened?" he asked.

"I was following you and the ghost came after me!"

"Ghost?"

"Ellen," she said. And she turned to the bushes. "She came from over there."

Geoffrey gave her a look of disbelief and then went across to the bushes to search. He was only gone a moment or so before he came back to her.

He said, "There's no one there."

"How do you find a ghost?" she asked bleakly, clutching her robe around her against the cool of the night.

Her handsome husband showed annoyance. "You shouldn't have followed me out here. I almost caught up with that fellow but when you called I gave up and came back."

"I'm sorry."

"Thanks to you he escaped."

"I didn't mean to make a mess of things," she apologized. "I called out instinctively."

Geoffrey said, "It may have been him. He

could have circled back and come out of the bushes to attack you."

"I saw the figure. It was a woman. The same ghostly creature I saw before."

"Let's go back inside," he said. "You're shivering." He placed an arm around her and they went back into the house.

"We couldn't have awakened anyone," she said as they entered the silent foyer.

"Be thankful for that," he said as he closed the door. "At least we'll be spared awkward explanations."

Back in their room she got in bed at once to try and fight the chill. Geoffrey busied himself at the sideboard and after a few moments came to her with a modest glass of whiskey in his hand.

"Take that," he told her. "It will help the chill. I'm having one."

She made a wry face. "I dislike the taste of it so."

"Consider it medicine," he said, making her take the glass.

She sipped it and gave him a forlorn look. "Do you really think it will help?"

"Bound to," he said, sitting on the side of the bed and drinking from his own glass.

She took another sip of the burning liquid. Then she asked, "Did you get a good look at whoever it was?"

"No. It was just a shadow fleeing in the dark. I couldn't make much more than that out."

"Could it have been the tramp character others have seen prowling about the grounds?"

"I doubt it," he said. "I'd say this fellow was well-dressed."

"I think so," she agreed. "Though I had only the briefest look at him."

"He went towards the beach."

She studied her husband and noted his frustrated mood. "You think it was the man who posed as Drake Winslow?"

"Probably."

"What do you suppose he is up to?"

"An interesting question," her husband said. "I wish I knew. First, the tramp and now this man lurking around. We'll not be able to keep help if they hear about it."

"I'm sorry I spoiled it for you."

He studied his empty glass which he was still holding and said philosophically, "As I had the choice between catching him and protecting you I preferred to take care of you."

"Perhaps they are working together," she said, a strange look on her pretty face.

"Working together? Who?"

"The two ghosts, Ellen and Drake."

"You have a fantastic imagination," he said.

"It was Ellen who came after me," she insisted.

He took the empty glass from her. "I say you were too afraid to really see who or what it was!"

"No!" she protested. "I did see her."

He went back to the sideboard with the glasses. His back to her, he said, "We'll not worry about it any more tonight."

She was looking up at him with troubled eyes as he came back to the bed and removed his robe before getting in under the sheets. "You persist in treating me like a silly child," she reproved him. "I wouldn't make up a story like that."

Geoffrey gave her a weary smile. "Get some sleep," he said. He kissed her goodnight and then turned off the light before getting into bed.

She lay with eyes wide open gazing up into the darkness and trying to make some sense of it all. The incident had thoroughly awakened her and sleep would come slowly. She couldn't understand why Geoffrey refused to believe her story about the ghost. If a thing didn't fit in with his preconceived ideas he refused to accept it.

But he couldn't deny the fact of the

shadowy figure of the man on the lawn. He'd chased after the elusive stranger and according to him had almost captured him when she cried for help. She guessed that it had either been the tramp or the man who called himself Drake Winslow her husband had been after. What had they been doing out there at this hour?

Events at Cliffcrest appeared to be growing more complicated with each passing day. And she still felt that much of the mystery revolved around the unseen figure of the famed poet, Ford Hunt. He was the key to many of the happenings and he could explain much to her if they met. Things she might otherwise never discover. It made her more determined than ever that the meeting should soon take place. With this uppermost in her mind she finally fell asleep.

The following day was sunny and warm. The fog which hovered in the area so frequently seemed to have disappeared for a little. After breakfast she went out for a stroll in the rose gardens to the right of the old mansion and found her mother-in-law out there with a basket and shears, pruning the branches and gathering some blooms.

Gertrude, a formidable figure, in a bright sun dress and with a wide-brimmed, floppy white hat featuring a broad black band on her head turned as Enid approached her.

"Ah, there you are," the matron said.

"Isn't it a lovely day," Enid enthused.

Her mother-in-law continued working with the rose bushes. "Yes. We get few enough of them." She gave her a sharp glance. "Have you done any gardening?"

"Very little. I've lived in the city so much."

"Yes. I'd forgotten."

"But I think I'd like it," she said.

Gertrude Hunt sniffed. "It takes a special gift to really do well. The roses haven't been the same since Ellen died."

"Did she enjoy the garden?"

"Yes. She spent a lot of her time caring for it."

Enid said, "I find it strange that a person of her type would turn to suicide."

The older woman gave her a bleak look. "You know very little about it."

"I realize that," she said. At the same time she considered what a cold person Geoffrey's mother was and how impossible it was to make friends with her.

"People have different sides to them," her mother-in-law went on ponderously. "You do and so do I."

"You're saying that Ellen had a dual personality?"

Gertrude nodded. "She was two people. And poor Ford was never able to grasp that. That was why they were so unhappy as man and wife."

"You think that was why they quarreled?"

"Yes. His refusal to see that she had a bad and a good side. Had he been more tolerant of her she'd never have been driven to that desperate act."

They were standing a distance from the grim old mansion and now Enid looked back at it. She gave a tiny shudder. "Don't you also think the house may have had some influence on them? It's such a gloomy old place."

Gertrude frowned as she used the shears to shape a rose bush. "I say that people control their lives. We cannot blame environment when we encounter that lack of control. Environment is only a small contributing factor. The character of people determines what will happen to them."

She listened to her mother-in-law's Spartan declaration without any surprise. It sounded typical of the older woman. She said, "I suppose in the final account it was Ford Hunt's jealousy of his wife which made her kill herself."

"He had every right to be jealous," the older woman snapped.

"But wasn't he unreasonably so at times?" she said. "I have been told that he was even jealous of the attentions she paid Geoffrey."

Gertrude turned to her quickly as if she'd suddenly pricked herself on a rose thorn. Her face showed anger. "Who told you a thing like that?"

"I don't remember," she said.

"Whoever it was lied," the older woman said in a rage. "Ellen had a frivolous nature but there was never anything between that girl and Geoffrey!"

"I'm sorry. I was only repeating what I heard," she said.

"You should be sure of your facts before repeating them," Geoffrey's mother admonished her, and she went back to her gardening.

Enid had no wish to continue a conversation which would probably lead to more arguments and biting words between herself and Gertrude Hunt. She'd about given up hope of ever being friendly with her husband's mother.

Now she walked further afield from the house to the very edge of the lawn. She glanced up at the attic and wondered what was happening up there. Geoffrey was probably working with the old poet, encouraging him to begin another day of creation. From what she'd learned she supposed that Geoffrey was a kind of glorified secretary to his famous uncle. Perhaps in the morning he would take letters and go over his correspondence with him. There must be a good deal of it. Francis James looked after the business affairs of the poet so that left Geoffrey free to cope with the purely artistic problems.

All at once she realized she was at the very spot near the bushes where the phantom figure of Ellen had sprung out at her the previous night. And as she turned to stare at the bushes her blood suddenly went cold. Peering out at her from the greenery were two malevolent eyes. Someone was spying on her from the shelter of the bushes.

As she watched the bushes moved and the eyes vanished. She stood there a moment longer and then began walking back towards the house with long strides. On the way she met the lawyer, Francis James, who was walking in the opposite direction.

He paused to ask her, "Is anything wrong?"

She nodded. "I was standing out by the bushes and two wild staring eyes showed in them. Someone was watching me."

"Did you get a look at whoever it was?"

"No. The eyes vanished and I started back here."

The gray-faced lawyer looked glum. "It's that tramp again. We've spoken to the police but it's done no good. He's been hiding out here on the estate for months. I think he goes into town occasionally or trespasses on some of the other families but he always returns here."

"Have you any idea who it is?"

"No," he said. "Just some old vagrant. But he could be a mental case and dangerous. He frightened one of the maids badly."

"I heard about that," she said.

"Be careful when you're out alone," the lawyer warned her. "I'll make it a point to get in touch with the police again."

"I think you should," she said.

The lawyer frowned. "When Peter was on drugs he brought all kinds of weird people here. I thought once he was cured we'd have no more of that kind of trouble."

"Is he cured?"

Francis James looked surprised. "He was discharged from the private hospital his mother sent him to. What gives you the idea he mightn't be?"

"He behaves so strangely and he's very nervous."

"That's a result of his addiction rather than a sign of his being on drugs now. In any case he was always a nervous person. That won't change."

"I suppose not," she said.

The lawyer gave her a sharp look. "Are you adjusting to things here any better?"

"I wish I could say yes," she told him. "But it wouldn't be true."

"That's unfortunate," the lawyer said.

"Yes, very."

"Have you decided what you'll do?"

She glanced toward the old mansion and especially the attic. She said, "Not yet." She noted the blinds still drawn at the attic windows and she turned to ask the lawyer, "Don't they ever raise the blinds in Ford Hunt's attic apartment?"

The lawyer sighed. "Among other things he seems to have developed a hatred of sunlight. It's just an extra eccentricity for Geoffrey to contend with. They work almost entirely by artificial light. The blinds are kept down."

She frowned. "It's an incredible way for him to live."

"I agree. But genius is unpredictable, especially when it becomes twisted as Ford Hunt's has."

"You're saying he's mad!"

"Difficult," he corrected her.

"I don't care how much money Geoffrey is liable to get out of this. I wish he'd find other work," she said worriedly.

"Ford Hunt's income has grown enormously," the lawyer reminded her. "I sign new contracts for him every day. Television, movies, the radio all want to use his new books. And that doesn't take into account the books themselves which earn a great deal."

She said, "Didn't Geoffrey do some writing on his own before he gave all his time to his uncle?"

The lawyer nodded. "Yes. Geoffrey had a promising talent. But I doubt very much if he'd ever have made any money. He wrote poetry like his uncle. And unless you have the reputation of a Ford Hunt it pays little or nothing."

"He might still be better off on his own."

"I disagree with you in that," Francis James said in his suave fashion. "You will benefit one day for the slight sacrifices you are making now."

"They aren't that slight!" she protested.

"I'd say so when compared to the possible profits."

"You think only in terms of profits, don't you?" she accused him.

He looked surprised. "I've never been accused of that before."

"I think it is true," she went on. "You don't care what happens to my marriage with Geoffrey as long as he keeps his uncle working to produce new profits for you and all the rest."

Francis James spread his hands. "That is my role here — why Ford Hunt employs me."

"Does he employ you?" she demanded.

The lawyer showed surprise. "I don't follow you."

"I mean is he any longer in his right mind? Is he sane enough to be said to employ anyone?"

The lawyer spoke placatingly, "Ford Hunt has become strange but he is certainly not mad. As a matter of fact he shows a shrewd interest in his business matters. Geoffrey takes the contracts and statements up to him. I often get them back with terse notations which are anything but insane."

"Where did he and Ellen live before her death?"

"They used all the house in the old days," the lawyer said. "Much of their time was spent in a sitting room on the second floor. He had a desk there and often worked while she sat near him reading or knitting. And their bedroom was the one you and Geoffrey are occupying now."

"I hadn't heard that."

"It's the best of the bedrooms," the lawyer said. "You are lucky."

"What is the attic apartment he lives in now like?" she asked.

Francis James grimaced. "No attic is comfortable. It is very plain and the furniture is shabby. But he does not seem to want any creature comforts now that Ellen is dead."

"Then he must have loved her a great deal."

"There's no question that he did."

"And she was less single-minded in her affections," Enid said. "You know about her and Drake Winslow."

"I know all about that unhappy affair," the lawyer said. "And Geoffrey has told me about your strange meeting on the beach with that fellow who claimed to be Drake."

"What do you make of it?"

"I'd say it was some practical joker but the matter is much too serious for practical jokes. I don't know exactly what he could hope to gain by pretending to be Drake."

Her eyes met his. "Unless it was Drake's ghost."

"Isn't one ghost sufficient for you? We have Ellen's."

She smiled wryly. "I came here skeptical about spirits. Now I'm beginning to wonder."

"I can understand why," the lawyer said.

"I saw Ellen again last night."

"You and Martha should compare notes. She claims to have seen her."

"I know."

The lawyer sighed. "I am also a skeptic. But you would expect that. I think one sometimes sees a ghost because one wants to. A rustle of wind or an unexplained shadow can do much to stimulate the imagination."

"Now you sound like my husband," she told him.

His smile was cold. "I'm sorry I can't be more sympathetic," he told her.

They parted and she walked on toward the house. She left him with the same feeling she nearly always had after they talked. The feeling that beneath his cool, calm exterior he was opposed to her. She would have a hard time getting him to show his animosity but she was certain it was there.

The house was dark and cool in contrast to the sunshine outside. She went upstairs and was about to take the corridor down to her room when she suddenly noticed that a door that was usually closed and locked on that level was now partly ajar. Some mental calculations told her this was probably the sitting room on the second level of the old house which the lawyer had mentioned. The sight of the open door made her heart beat more quickly!

Suppose that it was old Ford Hunt in there. She might be able to approach the poet and introduce herself, try to persuade him to give Geoffrey more free time or dismiss him altogether. Her nerves on edge she decided to approach the doorway and perhaps venture in. It was an opportunity which might not come her way again.

Very slowly she approached the doorway and glanced inside. From where she stood she could not see anyone but in another part of the room hidden by the door she could hear desk drawers being opened and papers rustling as they were handled.

She advanced into the room almost expecting to see the old poet but she was doomed to disappointment. For seated at the desk going through its drawers systematically was the hunchback servant of Ford Hunt's. When he heard her enter the room Watts looked up with surprise on his hollow-cheeked face.

She hastily improvised, "I thought it might be my husband in here."

"No, ma'am," Watts said in his raspy voice as he rose from the desk with a sheaf of papers in his hands.

"What an interesting room."

"It was one of Ford Hunt's favorites in other days," Watts said crossing the carpeted floor to her.

She indicated a huge portrait of a beautiful dark-haired girl which hung on the wall almost directly opposite the door. "That must be his wife."

"Yes," Watts said, studying the portrait with her, a strange expression on his thin face. "That was his wife."

"Ellen was surely a beauty."

"All of the servants were of that opinion," the hunchback said. "She was also very thoughtful of us."

"You must have been shocked by her death."

Watts met her eyes solemnly. "The manner of her death was what troubled us most."

"Did she strike you as the suicidal type?"

"Never."

"And yet she took her own life."

Watts was staring at the portrait again. He

said, "Her life was ended by a fall from the balcony railing."

She stared at the little drab man with his twisted body and it struck her that he had some very definite opinions as to what had happened and they were not in line with the accounts she'd heard.

She said, "Are you suggesting she wasn't a suicide?"

He looked at her calmly. "Her suicide was never proven."

"You feel it was an accident?"

"I think her death has never been properly explained," was his reply.

She furrowed her brow. "There were no witnesses so what you're suggesting is that the truth may never be known."

Watts was studying the papers in his hands. "It could very well turn out that way."

"There aren't too many possibilities beyond suicide," she said. "Accident seems almost ruled out. She must have been very familiar with the balcony."

"She was," Watts said.

She hesitated a moment before she said, "So that leaves only one possible other alternative — murder."

The hunchback nodded without lifting his eyes from the papers. "Yes," he said.

Enid realized she was moving on dangerous ground. That Watts might be deliberately leading her on to get her views. To report back to Ford Hunt or Geoffrey or whoever he was working for. Perhaps Francis James. But there was something in the hunchback's manner that suggested he'd been genuinely fond of Ellen and would like to see her death avenged. This gave her the nerve to go on.

She said, "Do you think Ellen was murdered?"

Watts looked up at her, the sunken eyes in the gaunt face enigmatic. He said, "I'm only a servant here. I know little of what really goes on in the house."

"I doubt that."

He looked away from her again. "My opinion can be of no value. But I don't think she committed suicide."

"Nor do I," she said. "Whom do you suspect of her murder?"

"I have no idea."

Enid took an urgent step towards him. "You must have some thoughts on the matter. You've been this frank with me you may as well go all the way."

"I wouldn't care to make a blind accusation," Watts said soberly.

"You mean you're not sure about the killer?"

"If she was killed," the hunchback said with a shrug.

Enid said, "You must help me. I need your help. I'm afraid to be in this house. I know there's danger for me here. And I'm sure much of it stems from the person who killed Ellen. If you know who it was you must tell me!"

Watts withdrew a little. "I'm sorry," he said. "You had better ask your husband."

Her eyebrows raised. "You mean he did it? He killed Ellen?"

"No," the hunchback said quickly. "I would be the last to accuse Mr. Geoffrey. I merely meant it is something you should discuss with him."

"I have and he won't help me."

"Then why expect aid from me?" Watts wanted to know.

She looked at him directly. "There is someone who can answer my questions and you can see that I get to him."

Watts eyed her uneasily. "Who?"

"Ford Hunt. I must talk with him."

The hunchback shook his head. "He sees no one."

"You could get me in there. Once I'm in the attic I know he'll talk to me."

"There's too much risk," Watts protested. "I would lose my job. My whole future would be threatened."

"I'll pay you well," she said. "You can fix it so it will seem I got to him by accident. You can think of a way."

"I don't know," the hunchback hesitated.

"Please!" she begged. "Get me into the attic somehow so I can plead with Ford Hunt!"

CHAPTER NINE

Watts listened to her urgent plea with a wary expression on his hollow-cheeked face. She felt sure she had almost won him over with her promise of money but it was fear that held him back. He was afraid of someone or something and so he hesitated accepting her offer.

At last he said, "Give me some time. I'll think about it."

"It can't be long," she told him. "I'm not able to stand things as they are. If something doesn't happen to clear up the mystery I'm going to leave."

"A few days," he said. "Maybe then I can help you."

"Why not now?"

"I have to talk to someone," the hunchback said.

"Can't you manage it today?"

"I don't know," Watts said. "I'll tell you later."

She saw that there would be no hurrying him so she gave up her urging. Better to let him come around to helping her in his own way.

She said, "I'll depend on you."

Watts moved his twisted body in a gesture of uneasiness. "I'll do what I can."

She said, "What did you know about Drake Winslow?"

The hunchback looked frightened. "I know he was murdered."

"He used to come here, didn't he?"

"Yes."

"He was a friend of Mrs. Hunt's, wasn't he?"

Watts nodded. "They were good friends."

"But Ford Hunt hated him?"

"I think so," he said. "I don't know."

"Everyone says so."

Watts looked frightened again. "I can't talk about that now. I have to take this material up to Mr. Geoffrey."

"What is it?"

"Notes made by Ford Hunt. He used to work down here. I guess he needs them."

She said, "Does my husband get along well with his uncle?"

"Yes," Watts said. "Mr. Hunt will have no one else near him."

"My husband should be making a writing career of his own rather than giving all this time to that eccentric old man," she protested.

Watts listened politely. "If you'll be kind enough to leave, Mrs. Hunt. I have instructions to keep this room locked."

"Oh, yes, of course," she said. "You will remember what we talked about?"

"Yes."

"And you will try and have word for me?"

"I will let you know," Watts said with such impatience that she knew she didn't dare delay him any longer. With a final glance at the lovely face of Ellen in the portrait she went out.

She could only hope that she'd made some headway with the strange Watts. The hunchbacked man undoubtedly had great loyalty to Ford Hunt and he would need to be convinced that her intrusion on his employer would do the poet no harm. He would also want protection for himself so he wouldn't be blamed for allowing her in the attic. If these two items could be settled she was sure Watts would help her.

Some of his answers had baffled her. And she still wasn't sure of his attitude towards her husband. It was possible he thought Geoffrey responsible for Ellen's mysterious fall to her death. She preferred to believe it to be the work of someone else or a true suicide. Eventually the facts would be revealed and then in turn other things would fall into place.

She was strolling slowly along the corridor when Martha appeared out of her room. The dark-haired girl was wearing an attractive rose linen dress of knee length. She came toward Enid with such a purposeful expression on her attractive face that it seemed likely she had news of importance.

"I was just going to try to find you," she said.

"Oh?" Enid was surprised.

"I'd like you to drive into town with me," the other girl said.

"Now?"

"Yes. We have a problem."

Enid was again startled. She asked, "What sort of problem?"

"Peter didn't come home last night."

"Is that unusual?"

"Very," Martha said. "He's always returned here at night. At least he has since he's been off drugs."

She gave the dark-haired girl a worried look. "You think it means he's started again?"

"I'm afraid so. I'm going to drive to the lounge and try and find out about him. I wouldn't mind having company."

"I'll go with you," she said.

"Good," Martha said briskly. "I want to start at once. Is that all right with you?"

"Yes," she said. "I can go as I am."

They drove away from Cliffcrest a few minutes later after Martha had a hurried conference with Peter's mother and Francis James. They all seemed badly upset by the discovery that Peter was absent. The general view was that he had gotten into trouble of one kind or another.

They were soon speeding along the broad expressway that followed the coast line. Martha had a grim expression as she kept her eyes on the road ahead.

Without turning, she said, "We could have done without this extra problem."

"I guess so."

Martha sighed. "When he goes off on one of these drug binges he becomes a little crazy. He'll do anything, say anything to get money to buy dope."

She said, "He may not be on drugs again. He may have met someone or just have decided to spend the night away from home."

"That's what we're going to find out," Martha said.

"You're going to the lounge where he works first?"

"Yes. He may be there. If not they may know who he went away with or even where he's gone."

"It's too bad," she said.

Martha kept watching the road. "It was bound to happen. Just a matter of time. Addicts like Peter don't reform. He's been off it as long as he could manage. Now we're in trouble."

"He'll do the most harm to himself."

The girl at the wheel frowned. "He could start talking. He has spells when he talks wild. We don't want that."

Enid listened with special attention. She began to realize that Martha was more concerned about what Peter could reveal about Cliffcrest and its people than she was about his welfare. Apparently Peter was a party to whatever dark mystery was associated with the old mansion.

She said, to test the other girl's reaction, "There's not much he could tell, is there?"

"More than you think," was the other girl's reply.

No more was said for a little. They came to a commercial section of the road with a welter of neon signs on either side of it announcing various cheap restaurants, motels, car agencies and bars. Martha pulled the car in before a long, one-story building with a lot of fake Italian trim.

"This is it," she said grimly as she brought the car to a halt. "Luigi's Lounge in all its drab glory."

189

Enid took it all in. "Pretty depressing."

"I've often wondered what made Peter want to play here. Maybe because it kept him in touch with the drug underworld. He knew he could always get it if he wanted it."

"Maybe so."

They got out of the car and Martha led the way into the lounge. Chairs were piled on tables in the dark, smelly interior as a big bald man desolately mopped up the tile floor. He halted in his work and gave them an annoyed glance as they came up to him.

"Joint's closed until four," he informed them.

"I know that," Martha said. "We're looking for somebody."

"There ain't nobody here," the bald one said. "I just told you we ain't open."

"I'm not interested in your customers," Martha said. "I'm looking for your piano player, Peter Hunt."

The bald man eyed them both with suspicion. "What are you to him? You his wife?" he asked Martha.

"He hasn't a wife," she said. "I'm just a good friend."

"Yeah?" the bald one stared at her.

"Yes," Martha said. "Where is he?"

"I don't know," the bald one said, leaning

on the mop handle. He jerked his head in the direction of a side door marked "Private." He told her, "You can ask Eddie. He's in there."

"Thanks," Martha said, and she told Enid, "come along."

They went through the door marked private and found themselves in a fair-sized office. A thin man with heavy glasses stood over by the window looking out. He turned to greet them with a look of apprehension on his pasty face.

"What do you two want? Who let you in here?" he demanded.

Martha said, "I'm looking for a friend. He's your piano player."

"Pete?"

"Yes."

"He's not here," the thin man said.

"Do you know where he is?"

"I don't keep track of everyone who works here," the thin man snarled. "What's it to you?"

"He's wanted at home. His mother is very ill," Martha said, lying with an air that showed she was no stranger to it.

The thin man hesitated. Then he said, "Pete got stoned last night. Some guy came in here and they started talking and Pete drank more than he should have. He wasn't able to play for the last hour before we closed."

"Then what?" Martha wanted to know.

The thin man shrugged. "I told Pete I didn't want anything like that happening again. And he went off somewhere with the other guy. Pete left his car here. I saw it when I was looking out the window just now. The other guy must have done the driving. Good thing. Pete was in no shape to get behind a wheel."

"You don't know where they went?" Martha said.

"Nope."

Enid spoke up, "What did this man who got Peter drunk look like?"

The thin man considered. "Never seen him in here before. Good dresser. Had a squarish sort of face and brown curly hair."

Enid said, "Thank you."

Martha hesitated. "If Peter comes back, will you ask him to call home? It's urgent."

"Okay," the thin man said. "I'll tell him when he comes in. But he's not due to play until nine though he's usually here around eight."

They left with this information. Back in the car Martha sighed and said, "At least it was booze. He's not on the dope yet. But where do you suppose he's gone?"

Enid gave her a meaningful look. "I don't know where he's gone. But I think I know who he was with."

Martha looked surprised. "You do?"

"Yes. That's why I asked for that man's description. It exactly fits the man I met on the beach. The man who pretended to be the murdered Drake Winslow."

Martha gasped. "Now it begins to fit!"

"What do you think?"

The dark-haired girl started the car. "I think whoever it was you met on the beach has more than a casual interest in Cliffcrest. And he's spent last night trying to get information out of a drunken Peter."

"Do you think he'll harm him?"

"I have no idea," Martha said, backing out. "But I'd better get back home and let the others know what has happened."

"You make it sound so serious!"

"It could be," was the other girl's reply as they started back along the expressway.

"Why should that man pretend he's Drake Winslow?" Enid asked.

Martha looked tense. "It might have something to do with the murder."

"Does he think someone at Cliffcrest did it?"

"Maybe," Martha said harshly. "Who can tell what that kind of lunatic might think?"

"He didn't strike me as a lunatic," she said quietly.

"Which proves nothing," Martha told her as she drove on. "I don't pretend to be any particular friend of yours. But if this is going to hurt Cliffcrest and we who live in it, you're as much involved as anyone else. We're in the same boat."

"I wasn't at Cliffcrest when all that happened," she pointed out.

"But you married Geoffrey," the other girl said with relish. "That gives you a share of any trouble."

"I don't see why," she protested.

"You will," Martha promised. "There are a lot of things you don't know about yet."

"I realize that," she said bitterly.

"If Geoffrey wanted to tell you he could," was Martha's comment. "Maybe he doesn't trust you."

"It's all you others," Enid exclaimed angrily. "I know you're against me. You banded together to be hostile to me right from the start."

"You are an intruder!"

"I'm Geoffrey's wife!"

"Geoffrey was a fool to marry at this time!"

"What do you mean?" she demanded.

"I'm only saying what I know to be true,"

Martha said. "You can find out the facts from your husband. Though the chances are he won't tell you."

After this bitter exchange they drove on in silence. They came to the private road leading to Cliffcrest and turned off. In a few minutes they pulled up before the front door. Martha quickly got out of the car and went up the steps to meet a strained-looking Francis James who was standing just outside the door.

"I didn't find him," Martha told him.

"I know," the lawyer said.

Martha went on, "He went on a drinking party with some stranger. Enid thinks it was with the man who pretended to be Drake Winslow."

Francis James said, "Peter has come home."

"He's here?" Martha exclaimed.

"Yes," the lawyer said. "A taxi brought him. He said it was Drake Winslow who paid him to bring Peter here. Of course the taxi man didn't know that Winslow was murdered years ago."

"I knew it was the same man," Enid spoke up. And for the lawyer's benefit, she explained, "I met him on the beach."

"I see," Francis James said looking uneasy.

"What kind of shape was Peter in?" Martha wanted to know.

"He couldn't walk by himself. The cab driver helped him to his room. I had Watts go get him ready for bed. He's asleep now and likely will be for some hours to come."

Martha gave the lawyer a knowing look. "It's hard to tell what he's been saying."

"We'll no doubt learn that soon enough," was the reply Francis James made her. "At least we know he's alive. And he's safely here. Anything out of order he has said can always be denied."

"Saying it is what causes the harm," Martha warned him.

"We'll have to talk to him when he sobers up," was the lawyer's comment.

The two went inside still earnestly debating the meaning and the dangers of Peter's drinking bout. She was left completely out of it. It was as if she wasn't there. She remained on the steps perplexed by the way they'd behaved. Rather than go inside she went out to the rose garden to sit for awhile.

She was sitting there going over it all in her mind and coming up with absolutely nothing when Geoffrey came striding along the gravel path to join her.

"I've been trying to locate you," he said, seating himself on the bench beside her.

Enid gave him a reproving glance. "I thought you'd be far too busy with Ford Hunt to think of me."

His jaw hardened. "We don't need that kind of sarcasm."

"It wasn't sarcasm, it's a fact."

"What's this about Peter?"

"Didn't Martha tell you? You're one of the insiders. I'm the only one considered an intruder."

"Don't be tiresome," her husband complained.

"I'm repeating Martha's words. She's a marvel. She makes use of a person and then turns on them. You missed a great experience in not marrying her."

"Let me decide that," he said. "According to Martha you claim the man who took Peter off on his binge was the same one you met on the beach."

"It's pretty obvious, isn't it?" she asked. "When the cab driver brought Peter home he said that Drake Winslow had looked after the fare. And Drake Winslow was the name that man on the beach gave me."

"Then it has to be the same fellow."

She asked her husband, "What could he be doing this for?"

"I wish I knew," Geoffrey said with a worried look on his handsome face.

"I might have met a ghost on the beach," she said, "but I don't see that it was a ghost who got Peter drunk."

Geoffrey gave her an annoyed stare. "This isn't a time to be funny."

"I wasn't trying to be funny," she protested.

"It sounded like it."

She said, "I'd guess that this fellow is interested in the murder of Drake Winslow and he believes someone living at Cliffcrest did it."

"He's wrong."

"He'll have to find that out for himself," she said. "So he's made a start by getting Peter filled with liquor to the talking point. And I can tell you're worried. All of you in the house are suddenly afraid."

"That's not true!" he exclaimed getting to his feet.

She rose to face him. "I say it is."

Geoffrey offered her an overbearing smile. "Now you're being childish," he said.

"No. I'm pointing out some truths. That man believes one of you murdered Drake Winslow and then probably murdered Ellen. The two were in love. She might have known enough to tell on his killer and so she joined the list of those marked for death. There is some link between the two crimes.

And I'm sure there is someone in this house who knows about it."

"Tell me," he jeered.

She ignored his tone to say, "Ford Hunt."

Geoffrey said, "I don't agree."

"I didn't expect you to," she said. "But if you'd let me talk to the old man things might be different. He might be able to help us explain."

"I'll talk to him," Geoffrey said.

"I don't think you will," she said. "I don't think you want to risk disturbing him in his ivory tower. You're afraid of upsetting your money machine. That's what you all regard him as now, a money machine!"

"Enough of that," her husband said.

"There's no other reason for your keeping him up there away from everyone," she said. "This is a crisis. And Ford Hunt should be brought into it."

"You don't understand."

"You keep telling me that!"

"Because it's true," Geoffrey said. "You'll listen to any stranger but when I try to talk to you it's a different story. You scoff at everything I say."

"I could tell you the same thing," she said.

Her husband's handsome face showed defeat. "There's no point in my trying to reason with you," he said. And he turned and walked away from her.

It was about what she'd expected. Whatever guilty secret they all shared they were unwilling to let her find out about it. They didn't trust her and she was sure Martha had on at least two occasions attempted to cause her death in an accident. There was no point in her remaining at Cliffcrest unless she wanted to court death. And yet she couldn't bring herself to leave. Not now when she might soon learn what sinister force had brought all this to pass.

She spent most of the afternoon reading in the library of the old mansion. Ford Hunt's interest in Chinese art had led him to purchase a number of beautifully illustrated books on the subject. She reveled in reading some of these. While her own understanding of the various Chinese art forms was limited, she did know a little. And now the text of the very informative books increased her knowledge.

For a very short time it allowed her to forget the grim events taking place in the old house. But it was to be only a short release from the terrifying reality of her plight. She was reading when she heard a furtive footstep near her and looked up to see the gaunt-faced Watts.

The elderly servant made a sign for her to be silent. Then he came over to her and handed her a key. In a low voice, he said, "This is for a lock in the cellar. It is on a door leading to a circular stairway to the attic."

"I know it," she whispered. "I've been down there."

"The winding stairway goes directly to the attic."

"Thank you," she said again. "I'll see you are well paid."

"Remember, you didn't get the key from me," he went on hastily. "It was dropped on the floor somewhere and you found it."

"I understand," she said. "And I won't forget."

The hunchback nodded and put his forefinger to his lips again as a signal for her to keep silent as he made his exit. She sat with a book in her hands for a suitable period before rising from her chair.

Then she left the library and made her way to the corridor with the door which led to the cellar stairs. She was tense as she clutched the key in her hand and started down the stairs.

She first arrived in the gray walled storage room and from it she advanced on into the frightening darkness of the larger expanse of cellar. Here it was always night and she groped her way towards the distant end of it with difficulty. Every so often she stumbled against something. And she wished that she had waited to find a flashlight.

But since she had none she had no choice but to get along as well as she could without it. She was encouraged by the thought that once she reached the door to the stairway and unlocked it she would have at least faint light to see by. The darkness was menacing and she began to have visions of the phantom Ellen. The last thing she wanted was to meet the ghostly figure alone down there.

At last she reached the door. She had a bad minute when the lock refused to open at first. But she tried a second time and the key worked. She lifted the padlock from the door and swung it open. Once again the winding stairway in the stone tower was revealed to her. With luck she'd get to the attic this time.

She decided to close the door after her without attempting to padlock it. In this way anyone entering the cellar would not notice the door had been opened. Now she began to ascend the stairs. She was still terribly nervous and she began to worry about what it would be like when she finally confronted the recluse. Would Ford Hunt be angry with her? And if Geoffrey were there when she arrived would he try to hustle her out without giving her a chance to talk to the old poet?

As she pondered these questions she tried to plan some kind of approach. At the same time she continued up the seemingly endless stairs. As she neared the upper levels there were broken bricks and signs of plaster crumbling from the walls. But the stairs appeared to be safe enough.

The stairs kept circling around and she felt sure she must be close to the attic level. Then she abruptly came to a halt as she heard Geoffrey's voice. He was talking to someone who answered him in a lower, old man's voice. Her heart began pounding wildly. She was close to her goal. Geoffrey and Ford Hunt were up there in conversation — she had only to burst in on them.

Then she wondered if she should wait for a little. With luck Geoffrey might leave the attic or at least move on to another room. Then she could burst in on the old man when he was alone. Geoffrey would have no chance to prevent her from talking to the poet. The more she thought about this the better she liked the idea.

So she sat on the stairs and listened. The

conversation came to her only occasionally. And she began to worry about delaying her entrance. Her tension mounted and she thought she heard someone coming up the stairs after her. She was almost certain she heard stealthy footsteps below.

She even went down a little to see if there was anyone. But the circular nature of the stairway prevented her from seeing far. It was very silent again and she decided it had been her imagination. Another trick of her taut nerves. She was standing looking upward and listening when she heard a distinct sound from below.

The sound of labored breathing! Terror crept through her and she glanced down, her pretty face distorted by fear. And then up from the shadowed depths of the stairway came a horrible looking ancient. She knew at once it was the tramp they'd talked about. The derelict who'd been lurking around the estate, somehow managing to exist on stolen food and sleeping in the outbuildings. The madman who had attacked the maid!

Now he was sweeping up on her with claw-like hands outstretched. Concealment was useless so she let out a scream for help. But as she tried to scream again the tramp closed a hand over her mouth and with his other powerful hand dragged her back down the stairs with him. She struggled in his fetid grasp but she knew only too well she was helpless against his lunatic strength!

CHAPTER TEN

The tramp was dragging her back down the stairs to the cellar. She went on battling him and for a moment was able to utter another scream for help. Then his hand roughly clamped over her mouth once more. She heard him talking continuously to himself and uttering oaths as she struggled against him. They reached the bottom of the stairway and he began forcing her out into the darkness.

She felt there was no hope. She was weak from her struggles and on the verge of fainting. The mad old man would be able to do with her as he wished. Then in the distance she thought she heard Geoffrey calling her name. Everything was becoming vague in her mind and she didn't quite take in the significance of his cries. But apparently the tramp did. For he almost at once let her drop to the cellar floor as he hastily ran off in the darkness.

"Enid!" It was Geoffrey coming out from the stairway.

"Here!" she managed in a hoarse voice.

He came up to her and helped her to her feet. "What's been going on?"

"That crazy tramp! I came down here and he attacked me!"

Standing in the shadows by her, Geoffrey asked, "Where is he now?"

She pointed. "He ran off in that direction."

"He could be anywhere," her husband said with disgust. "There are two or three exits from this cellar. He probably knows them all."

Her hand was on her aching throat. "I thought he was going to strangle me."

"Were you on the stairs?" he demanded accusingly.

"Yes. I thought I saw someone come down here. I followed. When I reached the cellar I saw the door to the stairway was open. I was curious and decided to see if whoever it was had gone up the stairs."

"So you started up them?"

"Yes."

"How far did you get?"

"Not far," she said. "I heard someone on the stairs below me. It was the tramp. He attacked me and dragged me back down. It was then I began to scream for you."

Geoffrey's tone was curiously cold. "But you didn't scream or give me any hint you were on the stairs until you found yourself in danger?"

"No."

"That suggests you were on your way up to spy on me," her husband accused her.

"You're being unfair!" she protested. "I tell you I caught a glimpse of a figure scurrying across the shadowed hallway and going down the cellar stairs. That was what brought me down here in the first place. And when I found the door open what made me start up that stairway." She hoped he would believe her. It was her hope to protect Watts.

He said, "The door to the stairs is kept locked. How did it happen to be open?"

"I don't know. The tramp must have found a key somewhere."

"There's a lot of the tramp in this."

"He played a big part in what happened."

"You were idiotic to come down here," he said. "And I know my mother warned you that you were never to use that back stairway."

"You're expending all your venom on me," she accused him. "What about the tramp you let get away?"

"Like looking for a needle in a haystack."

"He can't be far away. He seems to continue hiding out here," she said.

"It's a large estate," Geoffrey said. "I'm not willing to search every foot of it."

"So my attacker goes free?"

"Yes. You were a good deal to blame for coming down here alone in the first place. You're sure you didn't find a key and open that door yourself?"

"I told you what happened."

Geoffrey took her by the arm. "That doesn't mean that I believe your story." And he led her across the cellar and to the gray storage room. Then they ascended the stairs to the hall.

Geoffrey's mother was there to meet them. "I heard wild shrieks from the cellar," she said. "What has been going on down there?"

Geoffrey's handsome face was grim. "Enid was attacked by the tramp down there."

Gertrude Hunt turned to her in angry surprise. "And may I ask what you were doing down there?"

"I was following someone I thought to be suspicious."

"It turned out to be the tramp," Geoffrey said.

"Him again!" His mother sounded worried.

"He attacked me and when he heard

Geoffrey's voice he ran off," she said.

Gertrude Hunt scowled at her. "You were not supposed to go down there alone."

"I know."

Geoffrey explained to his mother, "She was on the circular rear stairway when he caught up with her."

The older woman turned to her again. "You know that stairway is restricted. You are not to use it. I made that clear to you the other day."

Enid knew she was in an awkward spot. She said, "I became very confused."

"So it seems," Geoffrey's mother replied with sarcasm.

Geoffrey turned to Enid. "Finding your way to the top of those stairs wouldn't have gotten you very far. The door at the top is padlocked on the inside. You couldn't have reached the attic."

"I see," she said quietly.

Geoffrey glanced at his mother. "I'm going back down to take a look around for that fellow and lock the door again. You take care of Enid for me."

Gertrude Hunt looked concerned. "Be careful of that tramp. He may be armed and you know he's quite mad. There's no telling what he'd do if you cornered him."

"I'm aware of the risk," Geoffrey told her.

"I'll take care." And with that he left them and went back down the cellar steps.

His mother turned to Enid with a scornful expression. "You have done nothing but put Geoffrey in danger!"

"I haven't meant to," she protested.

"What your intentions are, I don't care," the older woman said angrily. "I know how this has turned out. Geoffrey has already taken too many risks to satisfy your silly pride."

"I'm not the only one concerned," she pointed out. "Everyone here is in danger as long as that crazy tramp is at large. When Geoffrey goes down there to try and capture him he's doing it for all of you as much as he is for me!"

Gertrude looked surprised at her outburst. "I don't agree," was her reply.

"I didn't expect you to," Enid replied defiantly.

At that moment the hunchbacked Watts came down the hallway. When he saw them there arguing he looked as if he wanted to turn and flee. He halted awkwardly a few feet from them.

Gertrude turned to him at once. "You have something to explain," she told him.

"Yes, Ma'am?" he enquired nervously.

"The door to the rear stairway in the

cellar was open just now," Geoffrey's mother said. "You are in charge of the keys. How do you explain it?"

Watts licked his thin lips and glanced in Enid's direction. "I was just looking for you, Mrs. Hunt," he told Geoffrey's mother. "I was going to report one of the keys for down there is missing."

"How could it be?" Gertrude demanded.

"I don't know," the servant said looking more uneasy every moment. "It is possible I may have dropped it."

"That would be gross negligence," Gertrude Hunt said.

"Yes, Ma'am," Watts agreed unhappily.

"I shall talk to my son about this," she warned him.

Enid said, "You can't blame Watts for accidentally losing a key!"

The older woman glared at her. "I don't remember asking you for your opinion."

"Still, I feel I should give it," she said.

Gertrude turned to Watts again. "If you see Mr. James will you tell him I want to talk with him?"

"Yes, Ma'am," Watts said and he turned and hurried away as quickly as his twisted body would allow.

Gertrude gave Enid a scathing glance. "You take entirely too many liberties around here," she warned her.

"I will answer to Geoffrey for any mistakes I make," Enid said. "Not to you." And with this show of independence she also left the irate woman.

She went up to her room and bathed her throat as it was still aching. There were black and blue marks on her arms and her dress was torn. It had been a shattering experience in the cellar and she still recalled the face and figure of the mad tramp with fear and loathing. The wild eyes and the bloated, beard-stubbled face of the old renegade still haunted her.

There was no question in her mind that he was demented. The stamp of insanity had been written all over him. His gibbering and his strange actions left no doubt that he was mad. Yet he'd been wary enough to flee at the sound of Geoffrey's voice. And he'd known exactly where to make his escape. He was completely familiar with the old mansion.

She felt that Watts was safe from suspicion. The worst they could think was that he'd been careless. She'd wanted to protect the old servant. She owed him a debt for trying to help her. But if Geoffrey had spoken the truth, getting to the top of the stairs wouldn't have gotten her far. The door up there was kept securely locked and she would have found herself helpless on the wrong side of it.

Still she had tried. And she had failed again. It seemed that her stay at Cliffcrest was marked by a record of failures. She had the feeling she couldn't afford too many more, that soon she must somehow get to the bottom of the mystery shadowing the old house, learn the secrets they were all so afraid of being revealed. If she didn't, she had an idea she would follow in the steps of Ellen and perish in some tragic accident — an accident devised for that purpose!

She moved to the window and looking out saw that the fog had returned to hang heavily over the area. The spectral fog! Out there in that gray mist lurked the phantoms terrorizing Cliffcrest. Somewhere in the swirling fog the mad old man who'd attacked her was hiding. And it could be that walking along in the shrouded gray mists of the beach was the man who claimed to be the murdered Drake Winslow. And last of all there was the cloaked ghost of Ellen surely lurking in some murky corner of the estate ready to make an appearance.

There was a knock on her door. She turned with a startled look on her lovely face. "Yes?"

"May I come in?" It was the voice of Francis James.

"Yes," she said.

The door opened and the gray-faced lawyer came into the room which was already beginning to show signs of an early dusk because of the thick fog.

He came across the room with measured steps, his manner grave. He frowned at her as he said, "I hear you just had a rather close call."

"I did."

"In the cellar."

"Yes."

The lawyer asked, "What made you go down there? I understand you claim you saw someone suspicious go down and you followed. I find that a very flimsy story."

"I'm sorry," she said. "It happens to be the correct one."

"Do you mind if I don't accept it?" he asked.

"I can't dictate to you what to believe and what not to believe," she said calmly.

The lawyer said evenly, "It is my guess you went down there deliberately."

"Then there's no point in my denying it."

"No."

"And?"

He continued to eye her coldly. "I'm

going to give you some advice. If you are determined to remain here you had better change your attitude."

"In what way?"

"You had better quench your curiosity. If you continue looking for trouble here you may find it and in a larger dose than you're able to handle."

She raised her eyebrows. "That sounds like a threat."

"You can take it as you like."

"Of course I'll tell Geoffrey what you've said," she replied. "I have no choice."

Francis James looked unperturbed. "I don't care what you say to Geoffrey. He already knows my feelings on this matter. You'll get no support from him."

She met his cold eyes with a direct gaze of her own. "Because you and the others are exerting pressure on him. What is the secret you're hiding, Mr. James? The identity of the murderer? The one who murdered Drake Winslow and Ellen?"

"Ellen died in an accident. She killed herself."

"So you say."

The lawyer took a deep breath. "Well, I've warned you. Whatever happens, my conscience is now clear."

"I doubt that," she said. "I don't think

you'll ever have a clear conscience again. You know too much about what has gone on here. You've been too much a part of it!"

"I'm not impressed by cheap dramatics," the lawyer said in his cold fashion. "I'm trying to do you a service for Geoffrey's sake. If you refuse to appreciate it there's nothing I can do."

He left the room as quickly as he'd arrived. It was all in shadows now. She stood there uneasily in the near darkness knowing she'd been threatened. It was a veiled threat but a threat all the same. She was beginning to suspect that lawyer Francis James might be the ringleader of all the evil around her.

She had a desperate longing to talk to someone. Someone who might be sympathetic. And she had no one to turn to! It dawned on her how alone she was in the old mansion. And then she thought of Peter. He was bound to be in bad favor with the others after his drunken binge of the night before. And he would probably be awake by now. If she could find him maybe he might be willing to line himself up on her side. It was worth a try.

She turned the lights on in her room and then went out into the shadowed hallway. She knew where Peter's room was and went directly to it. When she reached it the door was half-open. She looked in and the fumes of stale whiskey assailed her nostrils. At the same time she noted that the bed was empty. There was no sign of the errant Peter in the room.

Feeling once more frustrated, she went out and down the hallway again. She was on the point of returning to her own room when she decided to see if she could locate him on the floor above. She went up the dark, silent stairway to the next level of the mansion and staring down the corridor saw that the French doors leading to the balcony were open.

It gave her a strangely tense feeling. For this was the balcony from which Ellen had plunged to her death, a suicide or the victim of a murderer.

She forced herself to go down the long, dark corridor and find out why the doors were open. After her other unhappy experiences it took every ounce of her courage to make herself do it. She reached the doors and saw that a dishevelled Peter was standing out on the fog-shrouded balcony. She stepped out into the cold dampness and stared at his strained, thin face. His long hair was unkempt and he was wearing only slacks and a white shirt open at the neck.

She said, "What are you doing out here?"

He had been staring off into the fog in a kind of daze. Now he glanced at her with dull eyes. "I needed some air," he said.

"Why come up here?"

"The nearest place," he said.

"How do you feel?"

He looked at her disgustedly. "How do you think?"

"You must have drunk an awful lot last night."

"I had enough."

Enid said, "You surprise me. So few people who have been drug addicts ever drink."

"I drank before I took dope," he said. "The way I feel now I could do with a shot of horse."

"If you start that again you're really finished."

"I'm finished anyway," he said bitterly. "You know how I stand around here. And I'm really popular after last night. Geoffrey came to my room and gave me a third degree. Wanted to know if I'd talked too much!"

She gave a tiny shudder. It was cold and there was also something sinister about this tiny balcony perched so high above the ground and lost in a gray mist.

She said, "I don't like this balcony. It's

219

the one Ellen used that night."

"I know all about that," he told her with one of his twisted smiles.

Her eyes met his in question. "What do you know about it?"

"She jumped over the railing," he said, touching the wrought iron railing with his hand.

"You must know more than that," she said.

He shook his head. "You're making a mistake. I'm not drunk any longer. You won't trick me into saying things that aren't true."

"Who were you with last night?"

He shrugged. "I don't know. A guy who liked Gershwin tunes. He had me playing them for him all night."

"Had you ever seen him before?"

"No."

She said, "He sent you home in a taxi. He gave his name as Drake Winslow."

Peter's thin face showed surprise, then uneasiness. He said, "That's a laugh! What a joker he turned out to be! Making out he was a dead man!"

Enid gave him a wise look. "You know he wasn't just playing a prank. He had some reason for what he did."

"What reason?"

"I don't know," she admitted. "But he sought you out and he got you drunk. Deliberately got you drunk. Do you remember him asking you any questions?"

Peter hung his head. "I don't remember anything until I woke up in my room."

"Whoever he was he wanted some kind of information from you," she said. "The others are aware of it. They were all on edge when they found out what had happened to you."

"You think so?"

"I know it," she said. "And I haven't any doubt if they thought you talked or might talk they'd find a way to silence you."

Peter's eyes showed fear. "Did any of them tell you that?"

"They don't have to say it," she told him scornfully. "I could read it in them."

He looked some relieved. "You're imagining things."

"I'm not," she said. "They know you are in on the secret they're all hugging to themselves. They see you as the weak link. If you're wise you'll protect yourself."

"How?"

"I don't exactly know," she said. "You could be honest with me. Tell me what you and the others are hiding. What sort of dark crime you kept in the shadows these six or more years. If I know what it is all about I might be able to help you."

"Great!"

"What do you mean?"

He gave her a nasty grin. "That's a great approach you worked out. Don't they call it working on the guilty one's fears? Well, you have it all wrong. I'm not guilty and I'm not afraid!"

"You should be."

"I'll think about it," he said.

She decided to change the conversation. She asked him, "Are you going to work to-night?"

"I'm late as it is. Not much use my going in. Eddie will likely fire me after last night. I got drunk on the job."

"I'm sure he'd give you another chance. You ought to try to hang on to even a job like that. You need something!"

"Yeah," he agreed gloomily. "I do."

"Then pull yourself together and go in to the lounge. You can borrow one of the cars here. I'll go with you if you like. I'll drive one car back and you can return in your own. It's still in the parking lot where you left it."

The long-haired Peter showed interest. "Why are you so anxious for me to go to work?"

"I want to help you."

"Yeah?" His attitude was skeptical.

"I want to be your friend," she said. "Though you don't seem to care about being mine."

Peter was staring out into the swirling mist again. He said, "I could use a friend."

"Let me help you," she said sincerely.

He looked at her. "You're more in need of help than I am."

"I realize that."

"You're not afraid?"

"I'm afraid but I think I can control my fear. I want to try and fight it out here until I can get Geoffrey out of this mess."

Geoffrey's brother looked bleak. "You've got a small chance of doing that."

"I could do something if I only knew the secret they're hiding," she said. "Or if I could manage to talk to Ford Hunt. I'm sure he would understand and help me."

"You think so?"

"Why not?"

Peter said, "For one thing he isn't all that kind. He's not like those poems he writes. The old man is a lot different. Greedy and intolerant of everyone around him. I know him!"

"You don't paint a very attractive picture of America's number one poet," she said.

"It happens to be a true likeness," the long-haired brother of Geoffrey told her. "I'm telling you because I want you to be saved a big disappointment. Ford Hunt isn't going to be interested in your problems or want to help you. He never wanted to help anyone!"

"I still think he'd listen to me if I could get to him," she insisted.

"You won't do that. Geoffrey and Watts keep him protected from everyone. Since he lost Ellen that's the way he wants it."

"Did he care for her so much?"

"He was like any old man with a pretty young wife, she was the main thing in his life. She even counted for more than his poetry."

"And she betrayed him with Drake Winslow?"

Peter nodded. "I guess you'd say that."

"No wonder he is bitter."

"He was a recluse before that," Peter said. "He'd gradually stopped giving public readings or talking to the press. You could tell he was changing. What happened to Ellen only made the change come on that much quicker."

"I'd still like to talk to him. You could help," she said.

"How?"

"See that I get into the attic apartment somehow."

"He'd only shut himself up in one of the rooms and refuse to see you," Peter warned her.

"I'd like to try."

Peter stared at the fog again. "You'd better talk to Geoffrey about it."

"Does that mean you won't do anything?"

"Geoffrey can do more. He's closer to Ford Hunt than anyone else."

"Geoffrey has already turned his back on me as far as that's concerned," she said.

"Then you're in a bad spot."

"So it seems," she shivered as she agreed with him. "It's awfully damp out here. You should come in."

"I need to clear my head."

"Haven't you had enough air?"

"Not yet," he was staring off into the misty night.

"I'm going."

"Okay," he said. "Sorry."

"It's all right. I'll still drive you in town to work if you want."

"Thanks. I'll think about it."

"I'll be in my room. I think you should go."

"You told me all that," he said impatiently, his hands on the railing, and his back to her.

She saw that she was annoying him. That he wanted her to go. And not knowing what secret thoughts might be troubling him she knew she should leave. So with a final glance at his spare figure as he stood there on the balcony, she went inside. She doubted that he would feel well enough to go to work. And yet she was anxious to see him keep his job. Miserable as it was it gave him something to hold onto. If he lost it he might slide back into the drug groove again.

Still worrying about him and his upset state of mind she went down the stairs to her own floor. She felt that she had made a small dent in his armor of pride. If she could keep on and really win his friendship he might be willing to reveal what he knew about the dark business going on at Cliffcrest. It was a real hope. She made up her mind to continue working on the errant Peter.

She was on her way to her own room when she heard running footsteps on the floor above. She halted and listened. And then a shrill scream of terror rent the silence of the foggy night. She stood there transfixed, knowing only too well where it had come from. It had come from the balcony where Peter had been standing!

CHAPTER ELEVEN

Standing there in the darkness of the hallway she felt a dread certainty that she knew what had happened. Peter had gone over the balcony rail in the same manner as Ellen. He would be stretched out on the asphalt below in a crumpled heap now — further testimony to the evil influence of Cliffcrest.

She was still standing there transfixed when Gertrude Hunt came down the hall towards her. The older woman wore a dressing gown and seemed to have risen from her bed. "What was that scream?" she asked Enid.

"It came from up above," Enid managed. "The balcony I think."

"The balcony!" Geoffrey's mother's voice was sharp.

"Yes." She didn't dare tell her what she believed. That her younger son was likely dead.

"Who could have been up there?" Gertrude wanted to know.

"Peter," she said quietly. "I was talking to him a few minutes ago."

"Peter!" the older woman gasped in dismay and then ran for the stairway to the next floor.

At the same time Enid heard rushing footsteps above and the sound of voices raised in consternation. Rather than go up there she took the stairs down to the foyer in a kind of dazed state. When she reached down there the front door slowly opened and Martha came in, pale and shattered, looking like a frail ghost.

Her eyes met Enid's. Her lips moved without forming a sound at first. Then she murmured, "Peter!"

Enid went to her in sympathy. "I know."

Martha shook her head in stunned disbelief. "It can't have happened again! And yet he's out there on the driveway!"

"I know. I was talking to him just before it happened."

Martha stared at her. "Then you saw it happen?"

"No," she said. "I wasn't there when he went over the railing. But I had just left him and come down to my own floor. He was depressed but I didn't expect him to do anything like that."

Before Martha could reply Francis James came hurrying down the stairway. The gray-faced lawyer seemed in a very upset state.

He practically shoved them aside in his haste to get out. Geoffrey followed him and gave Enid a short, knowing look as he went by her. Gertrude followed them down the stairs slowly. She was weeping, a handkerchief pressed to her mouth.

Martha at once went to meet her, and placed a comforting arm around her as she reached the bottom of the stairs. "You mustn't give away to your grief," the dark girl counseled her.

"I don't believe it!" Gertrude Hunt sobbed.

"I know," Martha said, leading her away into the living room.

Enid remained in the shadowed foyer staring after them. She was still suffering from the shock of the experience. And she found it hard to believe that Peter had chosen to take his life so soon after she left him. Yet she'd known he was extremely depressed. There had been a despair in him she'd never sensed before. But he had not spoken of self-destruction.

She was standing there listening to the muffled conversation of Martha and Geoffrey's mother in the living room when Geoffrey came back inside. He came over to her with a drawn expression on his handsome face.

"I must speak to mother for a moment,"

he told her. "Then I'll take you upstairs."

"He's dead?"

"Yes," he said grimly. "No question about that." And he left her for the living room and his mother.

She heard a sound from the darkness of the rear hall and turned to see the hunchbacked Watts standing there. His hollow-cheeked face showed shock.

She asked, "You know what has happened?"

"Yes," the old servant said. "Dreadful."

"Where were you when the scream came?"

He hesitated. "I was in the attic on my way to do an errand for Mr. Hunt. I'd just left Mr. Geoffrey."

Before she could question him further the door from the outside opened again and Francis James came in. Seeing Watts he went to him. He said, "Get a blanket and a lantern. I want Mr. Peter's body covered and the lantern set out by it. And I'd like you or someone else among the servants to guard the body until the police get here."

"Yes, sir," Watts said respectfully. And he turned to vanish in the shadows.

Francis James gave her a stern glance. "I trust you're not about to indulge in hysterics?"

"No. I'm fully in control," she said.

"Good," the lawyer said. "Peter has been nothing but trouble for us for years. Now he's managed the crowning feat. We'll be subjected to police investigation and there'll be the usual gossip. We're just getting over Ellen's suicide and now this had to happen!"

"Do you think he took his own life?" she asked.

He glared at her. "Of course! He went over the railing and he's on the ground down here dead."

"It's horrible! His death seems so pointless!"

Francis James' lean face showed disdain. "I can't feel badly for him considering the plight he's left the rest of us in. I must go now and phone the police."

She watched him leave for his study and then she turned to go in to the living room where Geoffrey had gone to be with his mother.

But Geoffrey returned sooner than she'd expected. He came to meet her as she was starting for the entrance to the living room. His face bore the same tense look.

He said, "I'll take you upstairs."

She hesitated. "Is there anything I can do down here?"

"No. Mother is better now."

"This will be very hard on her."

"There's nothing we can do about that," he said. "Where is Francis James?"

"He's phoned for the police," she said.

"Good," her husband said with a sigh.

"Watts is out with the body so there's little to be done until the police get here."

She gave her husband a questioning glance. "What about your Uncle Ford? Won't he be aware something is wrong?"

Geoffrey frowned. "He is extremely deaf. I'm sure he didn't hear the scream. I barely heard it. He doesn't know what has happened yet and perhaps the best thing we can do is keep it from him as long as possible."

"The police will want to question him," she pointed out.

"We'll deal with that when the time comes," he said grimly. "To break the tragedy to him now would not be doing him any favor."

"Perhaps you're right," she said doubtfully.

"You don't know how remote he is from the everyday world," was her husband's comment. "Even making what happened clear to him will be difficult."

"You know his state better than anyone else," she said.

"I do," he promised her. "Let me get you

upstairs before the police arrive. You'll want to see as little of them as possible."

"I can go up alone if you'd rather stay down here."

"There's nothing I can do down here at the moment," he said.

They went up the stairs in silence. As she mounted the shadowed stairway she was thinking of the events just preceding the tragedy. There were those hasty footsteps she'd heard moving toward the balcony. She was certain they had come first. And then there had been that eerie scream from poor Peter. Whether there were retreating footsteps or not she couldn't be sure. But what she'd heard planted a certainty in her mind that Peter had not been a suicide. Someone must have deliberately pushed him over the railing.

As soon as they entered their bedroom she turned to Geoffrey with troubled conviction. "Peter didn't kill himself!"

Geoffrey's handsome face showed surprise. "What makes you say a thing like that?"

"I talked to him before it happened. He didn't talk like a suicide."

He gave a weary gesture. "Who knows how a suicide talks? The fact speaks for itself! He's down there dead!"

"I don't care," she insisted. "I heard steps in the upper hallway before he screamed. Rushing footsteps."

Her husband frowned. "You must be mistaken!"

"No! It was after that Peter screamed."

Geoffrey was obviously growing more and more upset. "You don't really believe you heard anyone running up there?"

"Yes."

"But you can't prove it. You didn't actually see anyone?"

"No," she said. "But I thought I heard footsteps before it happened."

He gazed at her grimly. "You thought you heard footsteps. And so you're ready to dub Peter's death a murder!"

"It may have been."

"We both know it wasn't. Peter was in a low mood."

"Not ready to kill himself," she protested.

He was facing her and rather angry. "How can you be so sure?"

She hesitated. "I can't."

"Then don't make wild accusations," her husband advised. "We're going to have enough unpleasantness here as it is. Don't try to make it worse."

"But you want the truth to come out!"

"The truth will come out," he assured her.

"I should tell my story to the police."

"No!"

"But how can they decide what happened without all the facts?"

"They'll make their investigation," he promised her. "They are competent."

She looked at him with shocked disbelief. "You don't want me to say anything about it."

"No!" His answer was emphatic.

"But that's wrong!"

"Not really," he said. "You want to tell them something which you are not able to substantiate. It could cause a lot of extra trouble here without producing any results. If you had seen someone or were more certain about this I'd go along with it. I can't as things are."

She tried to see it his way but she was tormented by doubts. She said, "What wrong could come of my telling the police about the footsteps?"

"They'd decide it might have been murder. They'd do a lot of digging. Bring up all the business of Ellen again!"

"And you don't want that?"

Geoffrey's handsome face was pale. "We're just living down that scandal. Why start another? This suicide is bad enough, why make it worse?"

"I liked Peter even though I didn't get to know him well," she said. "I don't enjoy thinking he may have been murdered and not doing anything about it."

"I understand Peter better than you," he said. "He tried to kill himself several times before."

"No one mentioned that to me."

"It's not a thing to talk about. But you did know he'd been a drug addict. He also drank. And last night he was on a binge."

"I know."

"The circumstances were right for his suicide. He was at the end of his rope. I have no question that he did it himself."

Her eyes searched his solemnly. "What about the footsteps?"

"They could have been his," Geoffrey said. "He might have felt the impulse to throw himself over the railing taking hold of him and so dragged himself away from the balcony. He could have raced down the hall in a panic, then given way to his suicidal impulses again and gone through with killing himself."

She listened and knew he could be right. She'd not thought about it this way before. There was a good chance that the footsteps she'd heard had been Peter's own. No doubt the police would eventually come to the same conclusion. Geoffrey was probably right. It might be better not to say anything about them.

She said, "Perhaps you're right."

"I know I am," he said, relieved. "When the police question you tell them everything, including your conversation with Peter, and where you were when it happened. But don't feed them with a lot of suppositions."

"I won't," she promised.

"Good girl," he drew her close to him and kissed her on the forehead. Then he said, "I'm going downstairs now and wait for the police with Francis James."

"You'll call me when I'm needed?"

"Yes."

"You're sure there's nothing I can do for your mother?"

"Nothing," he said. "Martha understands her. And Mother must have been expecting something like this for a long while. She has gone through a lot with Peter."

"I know."

He frowned. "I'm not going near Uncle Ford until after I've had a talk with the police," he said. "This is going to be harder on him than anyone else when he finds out about it. He is not well to begin with."

She saw her husband to the door and then

returned to her room to pace up and down nervously. She hoped that she was doing right. Geoffrey's very logical reason for not telling the police had convinced her it would be unwise. What had bothered her was his mention that Peter's death by suicide might be linked with Ellen's if she had brought up the subject of murder.

Did that mean Geoffrey still secretly believed Ellen had been murdered? And if so, by whom? And could the same person also be guilty of Peter's death? And if you wanted to go all the way back, why not Drake Winslow's as well? It was a shattering thought and it brought her to a standstill in the middle of the room.

For with it came another dreadful thought. If Geoffrey were so anxious to protect the killer who could the killer be? And the answer was only too obvious! The person he'd be most dedicated to protecting would surely be himself! He could be the triple-murderer! And that might be why he was so anxious for her to say nothing about the footsteps to the police. He didn't want a chain of investigations begun which might ultimately lead to him.

Her husband a murderer!

It was a shocking possibility but one she'd considered before. So it was really not all that new to her. But now it seemed so much more likely. And yet it could all be a tempest of doubt in her mind. She would do well to consider before going against Geoffrey's wishes. Better to go along with him until she was more sure of her facts. Or at least until something happened to make her suspect that Geoffrey or someone else in the old mansion might be the killer.

And what about poor old Ford Hunt? The unhappy recluse still unaware of the new complications that had come to them. Living up in that remote attic above the hatreds and turmoil of Cliffcrest. It would appear that he soon would have to be informed about his nephew's sudden death.

The sound of the siren on the approaching police car brought her quickly out of her reverie. And she steeled herself for the interview that would be sure to follow the arrival of the police. There would be the others to question and so she would have a while.

That night remained in her memory like a bad dream. Things were confused and distorted in her recollections of it. She recalled the grave-faced state trooper as he questioned her and took down her answers. Geoffrey had stood by all the while with a strained look on his face. She'd done exactly what he'd requested and not said anything about the footsteps.

She could tell by the policeman's manner that he was ready to give them a clean bill of health on the incident. As he closed his notebook he thanked her politely and turned to Geoffrey with the suggestion that there was little question Peter had been a suicide. And nothing changed in the days that followed.

Enid found herself in a desperately troubled mood. But nothing had turned up to justify her changing her story to the police. The fog came in again heavily and seemed reluctant to leave the tiny point of land jutting out into the Pacific. Its dreary gray was a clue to the tone of the feelings of the people in the old mansion.

Peter was buried in the family lot in a cemetery not too far from Cliffcrest. As the coffin was lowered into the ground Gertrude Hunt sobbed loudly but a glance at Geoffrey's handsome face showed no emotion there beyond perhaps a mild satisfaction. Martha stood by the grave, pale and wan, while Francis James had never appeared more grim.

The ancient poet, Ford Hunt, did not turn up at the funeral. Again he had refused to leave his attic retreat though he had sent a large floral contribution to be placed on the grave. The old man had escaped most of the unpleasantness of Peter's suicide. At Geoffrey's request the police had not bothered to question him. In his deaf state and sequestered up in the attic he had no knowledge of what had gone on below. It had been the humane thing to spare him any third degree about the night.

As they left the cemetery Enid worried about what would happen at Cliffcrest next. How long could the tense state of things continue in the old mansion? For the feeling that they were all concealing some dark secret had only grown with the tragic death of Peter.

The evening after the funeral the house was strangely silent. There was not even the usual brisk conversation at the dinner table. And the hunchback, Watts, glided about the mansion like a troubled wraith. Enid found little to say to anyone, including her husband. She still felt that the best thing for them would be to leave Cliffcrest. But since she knew Geoffrey would never agree she didn't bring it up.

Geoffrey spent even longer hours in the attic with his famed uncle. When she tried to discuss this with him he brushed her off. Finally, in desperation, she went to the office of lawyer James on the ground floor of the old mansion and confronted him at his desk.

She said, "Why must Geoffrey be with Ford Hunt for such long periods these days?"

The lawyer sat back in his chair. "His uncle is very weak."

"I realize he isn't well."

"And to complicate matters a book of his is due at the publisher's," the lawyer said. "It was delayed by Peter's tragic suicide and now it must be rushed. Ford Hunt needs a great deal of assistance from your husband if the book is to be completed at all."

"Couldn't someone else help him? A secretary or someone of that sort?" Enid wondered.

"Definitely not," the lawyer said. "A secretary would only bother the old man. He is used to working with Geoffrey and again, I don't think Ford Hunt would have a stranger around him."

"I'm alone so much!"

"I know," the lawyer agreed as he got up and came around to stand by her with a sympathetic air. "But this is only a temporary situation. And the money that comes from this book of poems will one day mean something to you and Geoffrey. The old man won't live forever."

She gave him a reproving look. "You seem a good deal more interested in the money from the book than in the fact it will add to Ford Hunt's work and reputation."

"I'm well aware of that also," he said at once. "But I thought I should point out the practical side of your sacrifices."

"It seems Ford Hunt is always facing deadlines and Geoffrey is taking the brunt of them."

"The old man counts on him. And now that Peter is dead Geoffrey will be his chief heir."

"Does the old man know about Peter?"

"Yes. We broke it to him gently. If he'd had to see the police at the time of the suicide it might have been tragic for him."

"I suppose you could tell him in a different way."

"Exactly," he said.

"Still, I wonder."

"You wonder what?" he asked, studying her intently. "You don't seem too pleased with the turn of events. May I ask why?"

"Nothing, really."

"There must be something," he insisted. "As the family legal advisor I'd appreciate your being frank with me."

She looked at him directly. "I heard footsteps that night in the hall above. I keep worrying that someone might have shoved Peter over the railing."

The gray face of the lawyer looked grayer than ever. "Have you discussed this with your husband?"

"Yes," she said with a sigh. "As usual, Geoffrey thinks I'm wrong."

"Maybe you are."

"Maybe."

Francis James pursed his lips and then said, "As your friend, I advise you to forget all about this. I'm sure it amounts to nothing. And it might cause innocent people trouble."

"Perhaps so," she said.

"Geoffrey will have more time for you shortly and you will feel differently about things here," the lawyer said.

She left the lawyer feeling that she'd accomplished nothing. She'd known before she talked with him that Geoffrey was working with the old poet in the attic against a deadline. This was surely no news for her. And he'd told her little else.

Once more she was obsessed with the thought that she might be able to change the shape of things at Cliffcrest if she were only able to talk with the famed Ford Hunt. She knew that the old poet was the most important person in the house and felt that all the mystery and subterfuges going on there had to have their center in him.

Since Peter's tragic death she'd felt the menace of the old mansion more strongly than before. The certainty that its walls hid some guilty secret in which they were all conspirators continued to bother her. She continued to be treated as an outsider by the family and Francis James. And she felt this was part of it.

She again began to have thoughts of trying to reach Ford Hunt. These had been put aside after the shock of Peter's suicide, if it had been a suicide. Now she was once again eager to try and contact the Pulitzer Prize-winning poet.

With this in mind she went out to the kitchen and searched out Watts. Taking him aside in one of the small anterooms used as a laundry room, she queried him about the chances of his again helping her to gain entry into the attic.

The hunchback shook his head. "No, Mrs. Hunt. I can't risk anything like that again."

"There must be some way," she insisted.

"None that I know," he told her. "I'd like to help you but I can't risk my position here."

"I don't want you to do that, Watts," she said. "But you know all about this house and what goes on in the attic."

Watts gave her a troubled look. "I don't advise you to mix in what goes on up there," he said.

"But you were willing to help me before," she said, perplexed.

"I failed," he said. "And I put you in a dangerous spot. I wouldn't try that again. Mr. Geoffrey is very careful about the keys now."

"I'll pay you whatever you say," she told him.

"I know," he said, seeming to waver.

"Please help me!"

"Let me think about it," he said. But there was no true conviction in his tone. No suggestion that he would do his best.

She decided to go for a walk. It was close to dusk and foggy but she thought if she remained close to the old mansion she would be all right. She was familiar with the grounds now and being out alone at night didn't make her as nervous as it once had.

Putting on a trench coat and kerchief she stepped out into the damp, gray mist. She could barely see a dozen feet before her. It was a truly miserable night with the fog giving everything a ghostly touch.

Thrusting her hands in her coat pocket she strolled out across the lawn.

There was a disconsolate look on her pretty face. She seemed to have reached a dead end. There was nowhere to turn. No one to turn to. And yet she was unwilling to give up her struggle to save her marriage and find out the secret of Cliffcrest. She was a hundred yards from the old mansion now and she turned and stared up at the attic where Geoffrey was working with the famous Ford Hunt.

The lights of the attic showed through its drawn blinds as small amber squares. How different it would be if she could go up there casually and even sit quietly and watch the two at work. But nothing was permitted to her. She had no freedom of importance in the old house.

She turned away from staring at the attic lights and as she did so her eyes met a figure which sent a chill racing through her. Standing directly between her and Cliffcrest was the tramp who'd attacked her in the cellar. The renegade who'd been lurking about the estate for weeks. The same gray stubble of beard covered the ugly, bloated face. The madman's burning eyes were fixed on her. And then the dejected figure in the dirty clothes came menacingly towards her.

"No!" she screamed and stumbled back.

But he kept coming nearer, ready to grasp her with those powerful hands. She turned and with a scream ran frantically toward the hedges. She could hear the pad of his footsteps in pursuit as she raced on. She was running pointlessly, not really knowing where she was going. Only anxious to get away from the eerie figure pursuing her.

She found the sanctuary of the tall hedges, dripping with fog, but a welcome haven at this awful moment. She was gasping for breath and sobbing at the same time. Now she crouched behind the hedge and peered out through the gray mist to see where the tramp had gone. It seemed that she might have eluded him.

But she was not yet ready to brave the lawn, come out where he might see her and begin the pursuit again. So she stayed there like a cornered animal, her heart pounding with fear. In the furor caused by Peter's death the tramp had been forgotten. She'd not heard any mention of him lately but there could be no doubt that he was still hiding out on the estate.

She stared into the heavy gray fog and wondered how long she might have to hide there in that craven fashion. She was cold and miserable in addition to being badly frightened. She had an idea he was lurking close by ready to spring on her when she emerged from the hedge.

Suddenly even the small security she'd felt in this hiding place vanished as she was seized by the arm. She almost collapsed of shock and for a few seconds didn't dare to look and see who it was had crept up on her in this fashion.

CHAPTER TWELVE

"It's all right," a voice at her elbow said reassuringly.

She turned and found herself looking into the face of the man she'd come to know as Drake Winslow. His square face held a serious look but there was no menace in his expression. Like herself he wore a trench coat and no hat.

"You!" she exclaimed.

He smiled grimly. "You remember me?"

"Of course! You met me on the beach and posed as the murdered Drake Winslow."

"How do you know I'm not his ghost?"

"Your grip is much too real for that," she told him.

He eased his hold on her arm. "Sorry. I didn't know how you were going to react."

"I was terrified," she said. "I've been running from someone. An old tramp who has been hiding out here."

"I caught a glimpse of your tramp," he said.

"Where did he go?"

"I can't tell you that. He vanished among

the bushes over there."

"It's not the first time he's chased me," she said. "I'm terribly afraid of him."

"From the look of him you well might be," the young man said.

She stared at him. "What are you doing here?"

"I came hoping to see you and I was in luck," he said.

"I'm not sure I believe that."

"It's true."

"What do you want to see me about?"

"More than one thing," he said. "I have a car parked out near the road. If you'll walk to it with me we can drive somewhere and have a chat in comfort. There's not a bad roadside restaurant a mile from here."

"How do I know I can trust you?" she asked.

"I tell you that you can."

"And I've got to take your word for it?"

"I'm afraid so," he said. "It's not all that big a risk I promise you."

She glanced towards the distant lights of Cliffcrest. "They'll wonder where I am."

He gave her a wise look. "Will they really miss you all that much if you're only gone an hour?"

Enid hesitated. "I suppose not. They'll think I'm in my room."

"Then you'll come for some coffee and talk?"

"I'd like to know why you pretended to be Drake Winslow."

He said, "Come with me and you'll find out."

She worried a little as they walked to his car. What if he should turn out to be someone quite different than he seemed? He might be any kind of evil character. But she didn't think so. She was really gambling on her instincts in this. She felt the young man was to be trusted and so she was going with him.

They reached his modest black sedan and he opened the door for her to get in. Then he slid behind the wheel and started the car. He drove to the main highway and in less than a mile they came to the bright multicolored neon signs announcing the restaurant.

He smiled at her as he pulled the car up in the parking lot before it. "This is a Chinese place. But I'm not going in for food tonight. We haven't time."

"No," she agreed. "I must get back before I'm missed."

They went inside the dimly lighted, crowded restaurant and found a table in a remote corner. The music of the juke box would keep them from being overheard. He ordered coffee for them and then they faced each other across the table rather tensely.

"Begin," she said.

He studied her with wry amusement. "You believe in getting right down to cases."

"I need to. There isn't any time to lose."

"Where do you want me to start?"

"You might begin by telling me who you really are. I know you're not Drake Winslow."

"I'm not," he said. "I'm a reporter with one of the Los Angeles papers. What my name is and the name of the paper you'll learn later. I was sent down here to do a job."

She furrowed her brow. "What sort of job?"

"That's quite a story," he said. "My editors are interested in Ford Hunt and the manner in which he's changed in the past few years."

"Go on."

"They think there is something funny about it. I was sent down here to try and see him and do an interview with him as well as a full background story."

"But you didn't do it?"

"No. I tried to see Ford Hunt and was

told he wouldn't see anyone."

"That's true."

"They wouldn't even let me visit the house."

"It would have done you no good," she assured him. "I've been married to his nephew for some time and lived a good part of it at the house and I've yet to set eyes on him."

The man with the curly hair paused while the waiter served them their coffee. When he left the man leaned forward, "Who does see him?"

"Only my husband and a trusted old servant."

"Have they told you about him?"

"No. Only that he is very old and eccentric."

The young man stirred his steaming coffee and eyed her very seriously. "I came down here to try and do one story and I may wind up writing quite a different one."

"Please explain."

"When I discovered they wouldn't let me in to see Ford Hunt I decided to try and get some information about America's number one poet from some other people. The local people who sell supplies to Cliffcrest and the neighbors. I soon learned that Ford Hunt's change of character came about after a young man living in a cottage near him was murdered. A young man by the name of Drake Winslow."

She nodded, tense that this stranger might show suspicion of her husband. She said, "Some unknown killer smashed in Drake Winslow's head."

"Right," he agreed. "The culprit was never found. But many people speculated if it might not have been Ford Hunt. He was a vigorous man with a wife much younger than himself in whom Winslow had shown too much interest. The local folk whisper that Ford Hunt murdered the young man in a fit of jealousy. They say it changed his nature completely."

"It could be," she said.

"It's true he was married to a pretty girl given to flirtations, isn't it?"

"I think so," she said warily, sure he was going to question her about Geoffrey next and she was going to have none of it.

The man across the table from her sipped his coffee. Then he said, "About your husband."

"What about him?"

"Don't sound so hostile," he told her. "I'm not the police or anyone important. I'm just a harmless newspaper reporter."

"I wouldn't call you harmless," she said.

"I'm your friend," he said. "Or at least I want to be."

"You told me you were a dead man."

"For a reason," he said. "In my investigation all the evidence seemed to indicate that local gossip was right. That Ford Hunt might have gone to Drake Winslow's cottage and murdered him for paying too much attention to his pretty young wife. From that time Hunt became a recluse. And the local people claim his wife rarely left Cliffcrest either and she took on a frightened air."

"Their imaginations would supply some of that."

"Perhaps," the man said, frowning at his coffee cup. "Next I learned that your husband and this Ellen were very friendly. And it was only about two years after the murder that Ellen was supposed to have killed herself by throwing herself over the balcony of an upper room at Cliffcrest."

"So?"

"So it seemed to me that the jealous Ford Hunt might have committed a second murder. Genius is often close to madness. I know the old man is a genius but he is also human. If a young wife betrayed him more than once, isn't it logical to suspect he might take some sort of action?"

"I'm listening," she said, relieved that he hadn't suggested her husband as the murderer. His theory about Ford Hunt seemed entirely logical.

"And now we come to the third death, that of young Peter Hunt," the man said. "It is my belief that he was also killed by Ford Hunt for some reason, perhaps because he feared the young man might reveal the truth about him. Everyone at Cliffcrest must know he did those other murders."

She stared at him. "The guilty secret," she murmured.

"What's that?" he asked her.

"Nothing important," she said. "I was talking to myself."

"An interesting deviation," he said. "My contention is that they all know that Ford Hunt is a mad killer and because of his fame and the money he's earning these days they're trying to protect him. Peter was the weak link and so he had to go."

She said, "You could be right."

"I'm glad you see it my way. You realize your husband is as much a part of this conspiracy as anyone. And Francis James is probably the ringleader."

"What will happen?" she worried.

He gave her a warning look. "You'll probably be murdered."

His abrupt statement shocked her. "Me?"

"Why not?" he asked. "You're sort of an intruder in the house. Not one of them. They don't trust you. Sooner or later they'll decide you're on to them, and even if your husband objects, you'll be slated for death."

Her eyes were wide. "You're saying I'm living in a house of murderers."

"It amounts to that. They are all accomplices of a sort if old Ford Hunt is a three-time killer as I suspect."

"What can I do to save myself and Geoffrey?"

"The best thing would be to talk Geoffrey into turning state's evidence at once. If he exposes the killer and the others he might be given clemency. And the danger would be over for you."

"I'm not sure I can get him to do that," she confessed.

"You should try."

"I will. If you're sure you are right."

"Unless Ford Hunt is turned over to the authorities there are bound to be further murders. I promise you."

"He is so talented. His writing so fine. It seems a pity," she said.

"The man has to be mad," the reporter told her. "I'll stake my reputation on it."

"What do you get for your troubles?"

"A story."

"Is that enough?"

"Enough for me."

"What will it do to Ford Hunt's reputation? To his earnings?" she asked.

He shrugged. "That's a gamble. My guess is that morbid curiosity will make his sales increase for awhile. That people will read him who never looked at a poetry book. But in the long run his respect as a serious poet will suffer from his reputation as a murderer."

She gazed at him sadly. "So even seeing justice is done means destroying a great talent?"

"I'd rather destroy that talent than have him kill you and maybe others."

"You want me to talk to Geoffrey?"

"At once," he said. "Let me impress on you there's no time to lose."

She said, "Geoffrey spends a great deal of time helping him with his new books. He's devoted to his uncle. I don't know whether he'll do as I ask. He'll look on it as a betrayal."

"Then you can come back to me and we'll try and find another way. But you must try your husband first."

"You're a stranger," she said. "Someone out of the fog. Why should I put all this trust in you?"

He eyed her grimly. "Because you know as well as I do if you don't act now you'll be the next to die."

"I'd better go back," she said, moving her chair from the table. "It's late."

"I've probably kept you as long as I should," he agreed.

He called the waiter and paid the check and they left. All during the drive back to Cliffcrest she was plagued by the question of whether she should trust this stranger whose name she still didn't know. But she was convinced that he had the answer to the puzzle. That Ford Hunt had lost his mind and at least part of the time was a dangerous psychopathic killer.

The man drove her a distance up the private road, his headlights blurred by the dense fog. Then they walked the balance of the way to the old mansion. There were still lights on in various rooms of the main part of the house and in the attic.

He glanced up at the attic windows. "So that's his special retreat."

"Yes," she said. "Geoffrey is probably up there with him now."

The man's face was grave. "Talk to him when he joins you."

"Yes."

"You promise."

"I do. When will I see you again?"

"If it's a fine day or even if it's still foggy take a walk down to the beach around eleven tomorrow. I'll be waiting somewhere."

"I'm afraid to walk alone again. Afraid of that tramp."

"Don't worry," he said. "I'll be there."

She parted from him. And by the time she'd gone the few steps to the house he'd vanished in the fog. She stared out at the gray mist a moment longer and then went inside.

Suddenly she was more frightened than she'd ever been before. The things the stranger had told her crystallized her fear and put all her doubts in focus. This then must be the dread secret they were clutching to themselves. That the famed Ford Hunt was a madman and a murderer. That was why Geoffrey was needed up there so constantly.

The old mansion had never seemed more grimly silent or more menacing. Slowly she mounted the stairway with her shadow following her up on the paneled wall. She reached the landing and went down to her room. Inside she turned on the lights and began to wait for Geoffrey. But he did not come.

At last when it was really late and her nerves were taut she decided she must do something. She found a flashlight in one of the dresser drawers and with it in her hand went out into the dark hallway. The night seemed filled with phantoms.

Her heart pounded as she moved slowly along the hall to the stairway leading up to the next floor. She mounted the stairs using the flashlight to guide her as there were no lights on at this level. Then she came to the steps leading directly to the attic.

She listened, hoping to hear the voices of Geoffrey and the old poet from up there. But she could hear nothing. The eerie silence only served to make her more concerned and afraid. She decided to attempt the steps and try the attic door. She was about to start up when she heard the floorboard creak behind her.

With a tiny cry she turned and there stood the ghost! The phantom Ellen! In cloak and hood she stood there in the darkness. Enid somehow found the switch of the flashlight despite her panic and turned it on again. She focused it directly on the ghost and the phantom lifted her hands in an effort to hide her face as she turned to flee.

But Enid had been quick to spot the gesture. And now she lost her fear enough to fling herself forward and grasp the phantom who proved to be of extremely solid flesh. The phantom struggled to escape and screamed. Undaunted Enid reached for the hood and tore it off to reveal the rage-distorted face of Martha!

"So it has been you!" Enid gasped.

"You're naive! You should have guessed long ago!" the dark-haired girl said sneeringly.

"Why?"

"To frighten you off. What else? But you haven't even the good sense to be frightened away," was Martha's retort. "You'll stay here until you're killed."

"Martha!" This time it was Geoffrey who called out her name sharply as he came down the steps out of the shadows. He gave the girl an angry look. "So this has been your masquerade?"

Martha shrugged. "Don't offer me any lectures. I'm not in the mood."

Geoffrey confronted her sternly. "I'm not going to say anything. But I'll expect you to have your bags packed by the morning and I want you to leave before noon."

The dark-haired girl smiled sourly. "Do you think the others will approve? That they'll feel safe if I leave?"

"I'll talk to the others," he said in the

same angry voice. "Now leave me and my wife alone and get out of that ridiculous costume."

Martha smiled wryly again. "I think I played the role of Ellen very well," she said. And with that she went back down the stairs.

When she was gone Geoffrey turned to Enid and said, "I'm sorry. I had no idea she was doing this crazy thing."

"I'd like to believe that," she said.

"You may," he assured her. "What are you doing up here?"

"I was going to knock on the attic door."

"You know that is forbidden."

"I was too worried and nervous to wait any longer," she said.

"Very well," he sighed. "Just don't come up here again. Now we'll go to our room. I'm very weary. I've had a tiring night."

She said nothing to him about Ford Hunt, deciding to save it until they reached the privacy of their room. It had been a shocking revelation to discover that Martha had been pretending to be Ellen's ghost and why. She also thought it was certain Martha knew about Ford Hunt being the killer. She had even hinted at this when Geoffrey had ordered her out of the house. Threatening to tell on the group. Give their dark secret to the world.

As soon as they were in their room she turned to Geoffrey and said, "There's something else I must tell you."

His handsome face was lined with fatigue. "Surely it can wait until the morning?"

"No."

"Very well," he sighed.

"It's about your uncle, Ford Hunt."

Geoffrey frowned. "What about him?"

"I talked with a reporter tonight. He told me a lot of things. And he knows much more than you can imagine. He's working for a Los Angeles newspaper and I'm to see him in the morning after I talk to you. He claims that Ford Hunt lost his mind and killed both Drake Winslow and Ellen. And he possibly also killed Peter because he was afraid he might reveal his secret. The reporter claims you are all keeping the secret so he may go on writing and you'll profit by his work."

Her handsome husband stared at her with shocked eyes. "You believe all this?"

"I think so," she said gravely. "He claims that I'm due to be the next victim. That the others in the house think I know what is going on and they don't trust me. Martha hinted the same thing to me just now before you arrived. She told me I'd be killed."

"Martha's a little fool!"

"You are all mad," she told him. "You have made yourself accomplices through your greed. There is only one hope of your saving yourself and our marriage. You'll have to turn state's evidence and testify against Ford Hunt and the others."

He stared at her, his face now ashen. "You have it all thought out!"

"Yes."

Geoffrey's expression was derisive. "For all your intelligence you're wrong. You haven't guessed the truth."

"What do you mean?"

"There is no Ford Hunt! He doesn't exist!"

She was surely startled. "No Ford Hunt?"

"There hasn't been for nearly a year. He vanished. We think he threw himself over the cliffs. Anyway he's dead."

"Dead? But he killed those people!"

Her husband ran a hand over his thick hair and turned away wearily. "Your reporter friend was right in some of his conjectures. Poor Uncle Ford did go mad with jealousy and kill Drake Winslow. The police didn't suspect him or guess that he'd become insane. And then two years later he imagined Ellen was having an affair with me and killed her. After that we tried to keep him locked up all the time but he got away

266

one day. Watts saw him running towards the cliffs. His body is probably somewhere down there among the water and rocks."

"What about Peter?"

"Ford Hunt had been dead almost a year before that. So Peter must have killed himself."

She was staring at him, a new thought having come into her mind. "The poetry? Who wrote the poetry all the years he's been mad and since he vanished?"

"I have," Geoffrey said contritely. "It was Francis James' idea. The big money was just starting to come in. He didn't want to see it end and I was anxious to publish and get acclaim — even under my uncle's name."

She still found it hard to believe. "So all the times you've supposedly been working in the attic with him you've been doing the writing entirely on your own?"

"That's right," he said with a grim smile. "The growing reputation of Ford Hunt has been based entirely on my work. So in a way I'm entitled to the money."

"But you've been living a lie and covering up for a murderer," she protested.

"What does it matter now that Uncle Ford is dead?"

She eyed him with alarm. "What will the

end be? You'll have to own up to the truth one day."

"We will, later on, after we've made a killing," Geoffrey told her. "Can't you imagine it? It will be the literary hoax of the century! My reputation will be made by it."

"And what about the murders?"

His face shadowed. "No one can bring Drake or Ellen back. The killer is dead. What justice will be served by bringing it all out now? Ellen taunted poor old Ford into becoming a murderer. I'd like to spare his reputation if I can."

She had learned so much in such a short time she didn't know what to say. "I'm to meet the reporter in the morning. I'll ask his advice. I think you should see him as well and explain all this."

"I should talk to Mother and Francis James," he worried.

"Not yet," she said. "Martha knows too, doesn't she?"

"Yes."

"We'd better talk to the reporter before she leaves," Enid warned. "I have an idea she'll expose you in any case. Better to get his advice."

"Very well," he said. "I'll do whatever you say. I owe it to you for mixing you up in this. But I want you to know it is my talent that has made Uncle Ford's reputation grow as it has."

She went close to him. "If only you'd been content to use your talent honestly."

"I sort of fell into this," he said.

"And we must somehow get you out of it," she told him, gazing up at him tenderly. He took her in his arms for a long kiss.

It was a night of tension. She slept little and she heard her husband moaning once when he fell into a restless sleep. At last morning came. And with it another day of heavy fog. They had breakfast and she noted that Martha did not appear as usual.

She told Geoffrey, "You'd better explain to Francis James and your mother that Martha is leaving and tell them why."

"I will," he promised.

"I'm going to the beach a little before eleven," she went on. "I'll stay in my room until then. When I leave, I want you to follow me at a little distance. That tramp turned up and chased me again last night."

Geoffrey frowned. "That's something else I must do. Get in touch with the police about him again. There must be some way they can smoke him out."

"I'd hope so," she said. "He's a filthy old creature." She gave her husband a look of warning. "Don't tell the others about us meeting the reporter."

"Depend on me," he said. "After the chances you've taken I'm with you."

She went up to her room feeling relieved. And she waited there until it was time to start for the beach. Then she put on her trench coat and left. She lingered on the lawn outside the house a little to be sure Geoffrey would notice her leaving and follow her as they'd agreed. Then she began the fairly long walk to the wooden steps leading down the cliff face to the beach.

She walked amid the swirling gray mist feeling the bleakness of the day and of her plight. She was by no means sure she could save Geoffrey from disgrace. His part in the bizarre scheme was bound to come out and not everyone would be as sympathetic as she was.

She was nearing the cliff's edge when to the left she saw the bushes move and part and the terrifying figure of the old tramp come bursting out. With a mad grin on his bearded face he came straight for her.

She screamed and turned to run back. And as she did she saw the welcome sight of Geoffrey emerging from the thick fog. He at once took in the situation and moved quickly past her to make battle with the tramp.

But the tramp had halted at the sight of Geoffrey and now he turned and began running toward the cliffs. He was making straight for the edge at one of the highest points.

Geoffrey ran after him shouting, "Stop! Stop!"

But it was a hopeless gesture. The mad tramp ran straight off the cliff and with hands reaching up as if to clutch the air fell that desperately long distance to the ocean and jagged rocks below with a shrill, insane cry.

Enid had been following the two and now she came to stand at the side of a stunned Geoffrey. He was staring down at the froth-laden waves as they beat against the rocks. There was no sign of the tramp's body.

She said in a hushed voice, "He's gone! I wonder who it was."

He turned to her with a look of incredulity. "I saw his face. It was Uncle Ford. The famous Ford Hunt mad and lost. He must have been hiding out here as a tramp this last year when we thought he was already dead. That he'd jumped from the cliffs."

Enid's eyes met his. "He made the story come true today."

"Yes," Geoffrey said gazing down at the angry waves again.

She looked around in time to see someone else walking through the fog to join them. And she at once recognized the newcomer as the reporter.

He came up to them with a frown on his squarish face. "I heard some shouts and then I thought someone went over the cliff."

"Someone did," she said. "We have a long story to tell you."

And they told him the story as they all stood there in the fog. Below the waves beat a dirge on the rocks where the poet, Ford Hunt's body had dashed on the rocks.

The reporter listened to the story, then he said, "It beats anything I ever ran into. Ford Hunt was probably lurking in and around the house the whole time. He'd know every stairway and secret passage. I still say he probably killed Peter."

"Probably," Geoffrey agreed.

The reporter sighed. "It's a tough one. I just don't know how to start my story."

Enid said, "It would be kind of you if you began it by saying that Ford Hunt killed himself this morning. Throwing himself into the sea at the peak of an illustrious career. Since he's gone, does the rest matter?"

The reporter frowned. "What about your husband? And the others? They've made a wad of money on a hoax."

"It will end now," she said. "And by doing what he did, Geoffrey has lost the satisfaction of being commended for his talents. That's the most bitter denial of all for a person like him."

Geoffrey said, "I ask no favors. Print the story the way you wish."

The reporter looked down at the rocky shore shrouded in fog. Then he stared at them again. "What a headline this would make! And what a book! But I think I'll go along with your wife, Mr. Hunt. I think instead I'll write the tragic obituary of Ford Hunt. And mind he stays dead. If any new lode of poetry turns up to be printed I'll feel obligated to expose you."

"Don't worry," Geoffrey said, "from now on any writing I do will be under my own name."

"Remember that," the reporter said. He nodded to her. "Goodbye, Mrs. Hunt. Be sure those other vultures at Cliffcrest know our terms. I want you to be safe."

"I will be," she promised.

He sighed. "Well, I have an obituary to phone in. I must be on my way. Good morning, folks."

They watched after him until he vanished in the fog from which he had come. Enid felt a warm feeling towards this stranger whose name she still didn't know.

Geoffrey touched her arm. "We'd better go back and tell the others."

She nodded and looked up at him. "Will you tell them something else?"

"What?"

"Say we're leaving Cliffcrest to begin a new life of our own somewhere."

"Nothing would please me more," her husband said, and he sealed the bargain by taking her in his arms and kissing her tenderly. Then they resumed their walk back to Cliffcrest and eventual freedom through the fog.

We hope you have enjoyed this Large Print book. Other Thorndike, Wheeler or Chivers Press Large Print books are available at your library or directly from the publishers.

For more information about current and upcoming titles, please call or write, without obligation, to:

Publisher
Thorndike Press
295 Kennedy Memorial Drive
Waterville, ME   04901
Tel. (800) 223-1244

Or visit our Web site at:
www.gale.com/thorndike
www.gale.com/wheeler

OR

Chivers Large Print
published by BBC Audiobooks Ltd
St James House, The Square
Lower Bristol Road
Bath BA2 3SB
England
Tel. +44(0) 800 136919
email: bbcaudiobooks@bbc.co.uk
www.bbcaudiobooks.co.uk

All our Large Print titles are designed for easy reading, and all our books are made to last.